"Crystal...Jesus... It's been six years. My God, I've missed you."

Jack laughed and wrapped her arms around a six-foot-tall platinum-haired showgirl—the one female friend she'd ever had her whole life.

"Me, too, sugar," Crystal said, and burst into tears. It was then that Jack stared down at Crystal's hand...which was holding the very tiny hand of a very tiny girl with big brown eyes and long black hair. "This here's my little girl, Destiny. And I need you to hide the two of us. I got nowhere else to go."

"How bad is the trouble?"

"Ohhh, sugar...it's so bad I gotta tell you even your daddy and your uncle would probably think twice about helping me."

"You? You innocent in all of it?" Jack asked.

"Only thing I'm guilty of is loving the wrong man."

One thing Jack's father and uncle had taught her: friends stick together in times of trouble. She was soon to find out that they probably should have told her that a showgirl on the run is usually the worst kind of trouble of all....

Dear Reader,

We invite you to sit back and enjoy the ride as you experience the powerful suspense, intense action and tingling emotion in Silhouette Bombshell's November lineup. Strong, sexy, savvy heroines have never been so popular, and we're putting the best right into your hands. Get ready to meet four extraordinary women who will speak to the Bombshell in you!

Maggie Sanger will need quick wit and fast moves to get out of Egypt alive when her pursuit of a legendary grail puts her on a collision course with a secret society, hostages and her furious ex! Get into *Her Kind of Trouble,* the latest in author Evelyn Vaughn's captivating GRAIL KEEPERS miniseries.

Sabotage, scandal and one sexy inspector breathe down the neck of a determined air force captain as she strives to right an old wrong in the latest adventure in the innovative twelve-book ATHENA FORCE continuity series, *Pursued* by Catherine Mann.

Enter the outrageous underworld of Las Vegas prizefighting as a female boxing trainer goes up against the mob to save her father, her reputation and a child witness in Erica Orloff's pull-no-punches novel, *Knockout.*

And though creating identities for undercover agents is her specialty, Kristie Hennessy finds out that work can be deadly when you've got everyone fooled and no one to trust but a man you know only by his intriguing voice…. Don't miss Kate Donovan's *Identity Crisis.*

It's a month of no-holds-barred excitement! Please send your comments to me, c/o Silhouette Books, 233 Broadway Ste. 1001, New York, NY 10279.

Best wishes,

Natashya Wilson
Associate Senior Editor, Silhouette Bombshell

ERICA ORLOFF

KNOCKOUT

Silhouette®

BOMBSHELL™

Published by Silhouette Books

America's Publisher of Contemporary Romance

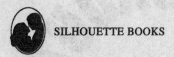 **SILHOUETTE BOOKS**

ISBN 0-373-51333-X

KNOCKOUT

Copyright © 2004 by Erica Orloff

Visit Silhouette Books at www.eHarlequin.com

Printed in U.S.A.

ERICA ORLOFF

is the author of *Urban Legend*, also published by Bombshell, as well as *The Roofer* (MIRA), and several books for Red Dress Ink. She lives in South Florida, enjoys playing poker and is an avid boxing fan. Her favorite boxer of all time, aside from Ali and Marciano, is the now-retired great featherweight Alexis Arguello.

Dedicated to three very special people:
Alexa, Nicholas and Isabella

ACKNOWLEDGMENTS
Thank you to the staff at Bombshell; my wonderful
editor, Margaret Marbury; my agent, Jay Poynor;
and the members of Writers' Cramp, Pam, Gina and
Jon. I'd also like to thank my father, a boxing fan.

Thanks to Lynda Curnyn, former editor for the
Bombshell line, for being a dream to work
with and helping me talk through this idea.

To my friends Kerri and Professor John—for the
memories of "clownlike" evenings.

And finally, to my extended family and friends, including
Walter, Maryanne, Stacey, Jessica, J.D., Alexa, Nick,
Bella, Pam, Cleo, Nanc, Kathy and Kathy….
I couldn't do what I do without you.

Chapter 1

My father taught me how to score a boxing match on the ten-point must system. He taught me how to throw a mean left hook, how to jab and feint, and how to punch—and not like a girl. He taught me to how to bluff in poker, when to hold in blackjack, and when to walk away from the tables in craps.

He told me, "Jackie, honey, never trust a man who's nice to you but treats the waitress like shit." He also told me you can count your real friends on one hand. And you stand by those friends when they're in trouble. But he should have told me, "Jack, a showgirl on the run is the worst trouble of all."

Which is why I was now fighting with my boy-friend in the foyer of my uncle's house, with a dead body in my bedroom, a little girl crying in my uncle Deacon's arms, and a welt on my forehead the size of a hard-boiled egg.

"You want me to *what?*" Rob squared off with me. It pisses me off that when we did have an argument, looking him in the eye was impossible. Rob was six foot two; I'm five foot six. Five and a half really, but I lie. He was also double my width, cour-tesy of lifting weights, and he had the build of a for-mer USC linebacker.

"I want you to look the other way while we take little Destiny to the ranch."

"I can't do that, Jack. I'm a cop—a detective. I do that and I lose my badge. This is a crime scene."

"Technically, it's not."

"And how do you figure that?"

"Well, I called *you,* as the man I sleep with. I did not, *technically,* call the police. So…if Deacon takes her out to the ranch, and you and I wait here for the police, all *you* would have to say is you never saw Deacon and Destiny."

Rob's gray eyes seemed to darken like two storm clouds. "You are *not* going to talk me into this."

"You know I am, so why don't you just give in?"

Rob clutched the sides of his temples and gritted his teeth. "Jack, the day I met you, my entire universe stopped making sense."

"When I tell you everything that has happened in

the last twenty-four hours, you will thank me for hiding her."

Rob looked from me to Uncle Deacon, to Destiny, and back to me again. He sighed with resignation. "Fine. Deacon, you can take the girl out to the ranch. But if after hearing Jack's little story I decide it's a bad idea, I'm going out there to fetch her back again and take her to social services."

Deacon looked over at me, and I nodded. I kissed Destiny on the forehead and whispered, "I promise we'll look after you." Deacon gingerly carried her in his arms, came back and took her backpack and things, and left the house.

Rob looked down at me and reached out to move my hair off my face. "You need to put ice on your forehead. You probably have a concussion."

"Probably. The room's kind of spinning, and I feel like I'm going to be sick."

"Yeah…well, my head's spinning, too. This story better be good, Jack. You have twenty minutes. Then we dial 911."

"Fine. And aren't you going to ask me to marry you?" Rob asked me to marry him about twice a week. We live in Vegas, and he just wanted to go over to the Little White Wedding Chapel and have Elvis marry us. But I told him I wasn't marrying him until my father could walk me down the aisle. And considering Dad still had four years left on his prison sentence, Rob and I looked to be semiengaged—I wore his pear-shaped diamond ring on my left hand—for a long, long time.

"No," he snapped, crossing his well-muscled arms. "I am *not* going to ask you tonight. Something about a dead body in my girlfriend's house takes all the romance out of it. Start talking, Jack. Remember, twenty minutes." He looked at his watch.

"Okay," I said. "Here goes."

Two nights before, I tried to avoid staring at forty pairs of perfect breasts. Naked breasts. As much as I tried to tell myself, "Jack, you've got two breasts, same as all of them," it was difficult not to stare as I made my way backstage at the Majestic Casino's show.

And actually, that wasn't true. I had two breasts, all right, but they most certainly did *not* look like any of the breasts on any of the six-foot-tall showgirls. Some girls have all the luck. Either that or all the silicone.

I knocked on the dressing room door.

"Come on in," Crystal's voice sang out from inside.

I opened the door and stepped into a pink nightmare. It looked like someone had thrown up Pepto-Bismol on everything from Crystal's velvet couch to the walls. Crystal sat, removing her false eyelashes—which looked like black furry caterpillars sitting on her eyes—and wearing a short pink silk kimono.

"Jack," she said, then turned around and flung her arms wide.

I walked over and leaned down to hug her. "God, it's good to see you."

"Did you catch the show?"

"No, sorry. I was at the gym until late."

"You have to come some night. The special effects are amazing. I actually fly at one point."

"I thought you were scared of heights."

"I am. But you know, the show must go on. Break a leg. The whole nine yards. I just suck it up and do it." The glitter on her cheeks made her look like a fairy princess.

"How's Destiny?" I asked, referring to her five-year-old pride and joy.

"Oh, just great, Jack. She's so smart. So cute. Here's her latest picture." She pointed and tapped with a long French-manicured acrylic fingernail at a photo taped to her mirror.

"Wow! God, I haven't seen her since diapers." I leaned in to look at the little girl whose long hair was pulled into two braids; she had big brown eyes and a wide, innocent grin.

"Yeah. She's getting big. A lot's changed, hasn't it, Jack?"

"You could say that."

In the nearly four years since I last saw Crystal in person, she had, as she put it, "really hit the jackpot this time," and fallen in love with Tony Perrone—the same Tony Perrone who owned the Majestic Casino, a television station, a fleet of planes and real estate from one side of the United States to the other—whose five-carat yellow diamond rock she wore on the ring finger of her left hand, though they had never got around to setting a date, and in whose twenty-million-dollar mansion she lived. He was listed in *Forbes* as among the top-500 wealthiest men in America. Under his tutelage, Crystal had undergone enough plastic surgery to transform her into a walking, talking human Barbie doll. She had also been taking French lessons from a private tutor, and after this season, would quit as the star of the Majestic's show to become a regular old Vegas housewife—albeit one who drove a Ferrari worth $200,000, had a private zoo in her backyard, complete with giraffes and Bengal tigers, and whose walk-in closet (more like a walk-in apartment) contained 862 pairs of designer shoes.

In those same four years, my father had been sentenced to prison for racketeering, after being framed by the slimy boxing promoter Benny Bonita, and I had moved in with my uncle Deacon as everything I once owned was sold to pay for my father's defense. Not that it did me—or Dad—any good.

"I have to talk to you."

"That's what you said on the phone, and that's why I'm here." I sat on a pink velvet tufted ottoman.

"Jack," she whispered. "The Mob is trying to get to your fighter, Terry Keenan. And if you get in the way, they'll kill you. They'll kill anyone who gets in the middle of it."

My uncle Deacon and my father were the only two brothers in boxing history to hold championship belts at the same time—my father as a middleweight, my uncle as a heavyweight. Together, the famous Rooney brothers owned a training facility for fighters nestled in the foothills of the Nevada mountains, and a gym in one of Las Vegas's less-savory neighborhoods. When my father went to prison, I tried to take his place. I was raised in a boxing gym and know as much about fighting as any trainer. Terry Keenan was one of our fighters, and in four weeks, on New Year's Eve, he was scheduled to box for the heavyweight championship of the world.

"What the hell are you talking about, Crystal?" She was nursing a white wine spritzer, which sat on her dressing table. Before Perrone took her away from me and all her friends, she liked Wild Turkey.

"Benny Bonita and Tony had a secret meeting. I heard shouting. Tony didn't realize I was in the wine cellar. I crept up the stairs and could hear everything. Every word. They have something on Terry Keenan. I'm not sure what, but it's big. They want him to take a dive in round five, and they don't care who they have to kill to make this fight go the way they want it. Bonita wants to take over all of your dad's fighters. Some high rollers and some big-time bookies want to see Keenan lose. In round five to be precise."

Crystal had serious conspiracy-theory issues. She thought everyone from Elvis to Liberace was beamed down in Area 51. UFOs, alien abductions, JFK, even Princess Di's death, if there was a conspiracy theory, she embraced it. Despite Tony's Pygmalion transformation of her, she still got most of her news from the *National Enquirer.*

"Crystal, Tony Perrone has a reputation as a ruthless businessman, and there are whispers about the Mob, but I can't see him doing business with the likes of Bonita."

Benny Bonita was the loudest, brashest, most crooked, most obnoxious fight promoter in the history of a sport with brash showmen—with the biggest pompadour toupee to match. He also framed my father, and I hated him with a passion. But as much as I hated him and wanted to buy into Crystal's theory, Tony Perrone was too smart. He would be careful not to have more than a hint of the Mob around him. It would be bad for business—bad for his gaming license.

"I'm sure of what I heard, Jack. Swear to God. Bonita said something like 'I should have taken care of the other brother—and that kid of Rooney's, too.' He meant you. That's when I panicked."

"Crystal, I don't know if there's any need to panic. This is a brutal sport. People do a *lot* of trash talking. It's part of the whole game. Put it from your mind. Keenan will fight Bonita's man, and he will win. And he'll win here in the Majestic's arena. I can't wait to rub Bonita's face in it."

Crystal stared at me, her long platinum hair falling to her waist, her eyes a cross between blue and green, perfect cheekbones (implants), perfect nose (nose job), perfect teeth (porcelain veneers). Surprisingly, only her breasts were real. "One of these days,

Jack, that stubborn streak of yours is going to get you in big trouble."

"Come on, now, Crystal. It wouldn't be the first time. And it sure won't be the last."

"You hope not."

"What do you mean?"

"I mean you just hope it won't be your last."

The next afternoon Crystal had shown up on my and Deacon's doorstep with her daughter in tow.

"We need to hide out here for a few days," she had said. Her Ferrari looked to be packed with expensive luggage. Her suitcases probably cost more than my entire wardrobe.

"Please tell me you didn't confront Tony about Benny Bonita," I said as I led her and Destiny into the house. She towered over me in the stiletto heels she always wore. We were a study in contrasts. She was tall, I was short; she was a platinum blond, and I had black hair with a lot of unruly curl in it; she had those blue-green eyes and mine were dark brown; and most of all, she had the build of a bombshell, and I had the build of a lean fighter.

"I didn't have to confront Tony. He accused me of eavesdropping. Said I was acting all weird. He grabbed my wrists and asked if I overheard him in his office. I blamed the way I was acting on the pair of panties the housekeeper found in our bed. She washed them and put them in my drawer. But they weren't mine. My ass isn't that big, the bastard."

"So which was it?"

"What do you mean?"

"Were you acting weird because he was cheating on you or because of Benny Bonita?"

"Benny. I've caught Tony cheating before. How do you think I got this rock?" she asked, waving her diamond in the air.

We retrieved her suitcases, and I showed her upstairs. Deacon's house was no twenty-million-dollar mansion, but it was a palatial luxury house. My bedroom suite had been done by some fancy decorator Deacon hired. He wanted it to be masculine, yet inviting, whatever the hell that means. My sitting room has a butter-cream leather couch and recliner, a French country table and Tiffany lamps. My bed is a king-size four-poster, and my bathroom has a tub big enough to swim in. On the walls and shelves, though, are *my* things. Pictures of my father when he was Golden Gloves champ, photos of me, him and Deacon taken from when I was a little girl and was hanging out in the gym, one of us at Disneyland, and one on a trip to New York City. On the wall hung my father's middleweight championship belt.

"So you left Tony?"

"I told him I wanted to get away. But really…I keep hearing him on the telephone, very angry, talking to Benny. I know he is. Tony's intense, but he's not a screamer. But that day with Benny, he screamed. Loud. Something's going on, and honestly, I don't want to be there when whatever it is happens. I told him I was going to visit an old friend and that I'd be back in a few days. I need to think this all through, Jack."

"Look, I'm no fan of Tony Perrone. He's got an ego the size of the Grand Canyon. However, you've said all along he's a good father figure to Destiny. And I still don't think he'd get involved with Benny in any kind of illegal scheme. Maybe the meeting was about the terms of the fight. About the arena. About percentages. About the cable rights."

"I don't think so."

"Well, look, my house—technically Deacon's house—is your house." I leaned down to look Destiny in the eyes. "I wish I had some toys for you to play with. I don't even have an old teddy bear. When I was your age, I was already going with my father to the boxing gym. I played with punching bags, and one of the trainers made me my own jump rope. But no dolls."

Destiny, wearing a pink backpack, smiled up at me.

"I brought some of her favorites," Crystal said, unzipping a big bag and pulling out a Barbie doll.

"You like Barbies?" I asked Destiny.

She nodded but didn't speak.

"She's kind of shy," Crystal said.

"I don't suppose they have a Boxing Barbie." I looked at Destiny. She giggled slightly and shook her head.

"One of our fighters has a match tonight so you'll

have the house to yourselves. Let me show you around. Here's the bed. You take mine—you and Destiny. And there's the bathroom. Clean towels are in the linen closet. I'll sleep in the guest room. This way, you two have the sitting room so she has a place to play. I don't have any food to offer you two, but tomorrow I'll get up early and go to the grocery store. All I have is leftover Chinese. And you know Deacon, he still does that juicer. You'll hear it whirring at all hours. You know that thing is strong enough to juice a human head, I think. If you want fruit, or raw carrots, I can bring some up. That's what he lives on. That and fresh salmon."

"We're not really hungry."

"Okay. I'll get some other food tomorrow. What can she eat?"

Crystal laughed. "She can eat the same food you and I eat."

"Oh. Well, what does she like to eat?"

"Pop-Tarts, chicken nuggets, French fries…Cheerios. She likes blueberry yogurt, the kind with the fruit on the bottom." All of a sudden, Crystal started crying.

"It's okay, Mama," Destiny whispered.

"Yeah, Crystal. It's going to be okay. Just chill for a couple of days. Listen, I'm going downstairs to let Deacon know you're here, okay? Why don't you freshen up or change into your swimsuits and go for a dip in the pool."

"It's actually time for *The Wiggles*."

"The what?"

"It's a *TV* show. Her favorite." Crystal picked up the remote and turned on my plasma-screen television, clicking through to the program.

"I didn't even know I had that channel on my cable," I said, shaking my head. Then I left my sitting room and went down to talk to Deacon, who was sipping some sort of brown-green liquid.

"What the hell is that?"

"Wheat grass."

"Gross. Hey, Deacon?"

"What?"

"Crystal's upstairs."

"Crystal? Well, Lord, it's been a while since we've seen her around."

"She's here with her daughter."

"How old is her child now?"

"Five. Listen, they're, um…I don't know. She's on the outs with Tony. Something's up. I told her she could stay a few days."

"If she needs money, help, we're here for her."

I looked at my uncle. He hadn't lost any of his thick black hair. His eyes were a warm brown, and his nose had a tilt to the left, courtesy of "Left-Eye" McGill, a boxer Deacon had squared off against a long time ago. "I was hoping you'd say that, Deacon," I whispered, and leaned down to kiss him on the top of his head, grateful for him. His given name was Nick, but he had found God somewhere along the way and became a minister by mail-order ordination. He was also the high priest of all things boxing, so the nickname fit.

I looked at my watch. "Dad should be calling in about twenty minutes." I opened the sub-zero refrigerator, which was very clearly delineated. Two shelves for Deacon, stockpiled with okra, kale, parsley, wheat grass, carrots and piles of apples to use in his juicer. Two shelves for me, barren except for Chinese take-out boxes, Coke and a bottle of tequila chilling on its side. I opened up various cartons of takeout, sniffing each one.

"This one's gone bad," I said, dumping it in the trash. "But I think if I microwave the chicken and cashews from Tuesday night high enough to obliterate any bacteria, I'll be okay."

Deacon rolled his eyes. "I don't know how it is you ain't dead yet. I can see your gravestone. 'Killed by Old Chicken.'"

"But I'm sturdy stock. Grandma lived until she was eighty-eight."

"I got my hands on you too late. By the time you came to live with me, your father had already turned you into a junk-food eatin', trash-talkin', poker-playin' hellion."

I gave him my best you-are-so-full-of-shit look. "Deacon, you play poker with me."

"Yes, but *I* do not curse like a navy seaman when we're playing."

I popped my Chinese food in the microwave, heated it and began eating out of the box. Ten minutes later the phone rang, and I ran toward it.

"Yes…I'll accept the call…Dad?"

"Hey, Jack, how are ya, kiddo? Good to hear your voice."

"I'm doing okay."

"How's Deacon?"

"You know, lecturing me about my taste for Chinese."

"Best food on the planet, especially the second day. What I wouldn't give for Chinese takeout right now."

"If I could, I'd mail you some."

He laughed his hollowed-out laugh. He was counting the days until his release—four long years from now. "How's Keenan look?"

"Good. He's in great shape, and Deacon says next week we'll go into lockdown mode, have him move out to the ranch. That way we can keep him from that flaky actress he's dating."

"Is she still talking about having a baby with him?"

"Yup. I'm sure it's a ploy to get at his multimillion-dollar take for this fight."

"He needs to dump her. He's too smart for that."

"Let's hope so." Both my father, who was a boxing legend himself, and Deacon had watched too many of the guys they trained fall in with, as Deacon called them, "fast women and phony friends." We all thought it was pathetic when people like Mike Tyson ended up declaring bankruptcy. Entourages, flashy clothes and cars. They bought into the life, and it ended up leaving them destitute with only fleeting memories of the good life.

"Want to talk to Deacon?"

"No, that's okay. Tell him that Keenan needs to stop leading with his left every time he's going to throw an uppercut."

"Okay."

"Listen, there's a line of guys here waitin' for the phone. Bye, Jack."

"Bye, Dad. I love you. See you next visiting day."

"Love you, too."

He hung up, and I felt my spirits sink. My father was framed. Sure, everyone says that whole "I'm really innocent" routine, but in my father's case, it's true. We even know who did it: Benny Bonita. Which was why, more than anything, we wanted Terry Keenan to win and decimate his opponent Gentleman Jake Johnson. We may not have been able to prove my father was not trying to extort Benny Bonita—it was the other way around—but we could plaster his fighter's face on the canvas and prove, once and for all, that the Rooney brothers—and one Jackie Rooney—were the best trainers and managers in the world. Even from prison my father was a better trainer, a better man, than the oily Bonita.

Later that night, Miguel Jimenez's face had the consistency of raw beef. He sat, shoulders slumped, in the locker room of the arena.

"What happened, Miguel? Look at you. You have bruises on top of bruises. You look like the friggin' elephant man!" I snarled.

"I don't want to talk about it." He wouldn't look at me, his dark black eyes darting away from mine.

"Oh, you're gonna talk about it. Something happened in that ring."

My uncle Deacon said, "Leave him alone. The kid feels bad enough he got knocked out without your big ol' mouth rubbing it in, Jacqueline Marie."

When my uncle uses my given name—instead of calling me Jack like the rest of the world—I know he means business.

"Fine. Just go shower, Miguel."

I shook my head and stormed out of the locker room. Deacon followed me.

"Jack, Miguel's just a kid from the barrio. He got an attack of nerves. He had an off night."

I wheeled around in the hallway outside the locker room. "That was no off night, Deacon. It was a dive. He took a goddamn dive!"

Deacon stared me down. Suddenly, I saw a flash of recognition go through him; his eyes changed almost imperceptibly. He shook his head. "My God…I…Lord, I think you might be right."

"And I know who's behind it."

"Bonita?"

"Has to be. You know, Crystal keeps going on and on about Tony Perrone and Bonita joining forces to take over our fighters, and she says they have something on Terry Keenan. They want him to go down in round five. She said she heard them. She's got this whole conspiracy thing going on."

"Yeah, but she thinks she was alien-abducted during puberty."

"I know. But she says she heard them."

"Why would Perrone mess with Bonita? I mean, sure, allow the fights to be held at the Majestic, but get involved? Get his hands dirty?"

"I don't know." I suddenly doubted the whole thing. "Maybe Miguel did just have an off night."

"Let's just go home and think about all this before we go confronting Keenan—or Miguel."

"All right. I feel sick to my stomach, anyway. What a lousy night."

The two of us had ridden to the Las Vegas Metrodome arena in Deacon's Mercedes. We drove out of the city of Las Vegas toward our home. I planned to try to get Crystal to think harder about exactly what she'd heard happening in Tony Perrone's office.

As we drove into our gated community, the houses sparkled with their outdoor lights twinkling beneath the Nevada sky. Deacon had taken his boxing earnings and endorsement deals he and my father did—a series of commercials for razors, and a popular one for Cadillac—and invested it all in Vegas real estate before the big boom hit. He had enough to live on in style for the rest of his life.

My uncle and father pretty much raised me together. Deacon never married nor had children, so it seemed as if I was his just as much as my dad's, the way he doted on me. He never fell for fast women and phony friends.

My father, on the other hand, had no phony friends but loved cheap women. He was saddled with me as a full-time father when my mother, whom he married in a Vegas quickie wedding, decided to divorce him equally quickly after I was born, leaving me behind, and moving to Hollywood with a B-movie producer she met while cocktail waitressing. I don't remember her, and frankly, I never missed having a mother, except when it was time to buy my first bra. Deacon and my father stood in the department store *arguing* over whether I should get the sexy black one (my choice—I wanted a boyfriend), plain white cotton one (Deacon's choice) or the sports bra (Dad's choice).

"Deacon, maybe we should have Big Jimmy around for Crystal. Just in case all this stuff she's saying is true."

Deacon nodded. I could tell he was still thinking about Miguel.

Big Jimmy was our cornerman and a former motorcycle club member. He was also Crystal's last boyfriend before Tony Perrone. He still loved her, I think.

As we pulled into our driveway, Deacon said, "I forgot to turn on the outside lights."

"Light's on upstairs," I said, nodding at my bedroom window.

Deacon parked the car, and we got out and walked up to the front door.

"Christ," I whispered. "It's open a little."

An uneasy feeling settled over me, and I looked at Deacon. Then we cautiously stepped inside. Two goons stood in the foyer, holding Destiny, who was kicking and clawing like a feral cat.

Deacon punched the one without Destiny powerfully in his sternum, sinking him to his knees with a loud grunt. I took aim at the other one, but he held Destiny up in front of him. She shrieked—loudly.

The goon Deacon punched was now leaning forward, almost to the floor, clutching his gut and gasping. I grabbed the brass lamp from the front hallway table and brought it down on his head. Then I turned and kicked the other guy in the balls. He doubled over for a second, then popped up madder than before. Sticking Destiny under one arm like a sack of flour, he reached out with his fist and tried to punch me in the face, managing to land a strong blow on my forehead.

But I didn't spend my life in boxing gyms for nothing.

I held both my hands up in a boxer's stance and ducked from his next blow. Then I delivered my own right hook to his jaw. Swinging around with my left, I connected with his nose, which spurted blood as he screamed in pain. He dropped Destiny, and I scooped her up.

Boxing is a sport of kings. And gentlemen. Apparently, no one told him the rule about fighting fair, because he withdrew a semiautomatic from a holster at his waist and fired several rounds as I dived for cover into the den and overturned the coffee table to protect Destiny and me. She was screaming again. Deacon tackled the gunman. The guy on the ground stirred and rose unsteadily to his feet.

"Give up the kid, and you won't get hurt," he shouted out.

"Fuck you!"

"One more chance…then you *will* get hurt. All we want is the kid."

Destiny looked up at me and clutched my arm.

I was trapped. I knew they would come into the den and shoot me unless Deacon overpowered them both. I heard fighting, the sounds of fists against flesh, and I peeked over the table. The guy with the gun was now on the floor, courtesy of my uncle, his gun clattering across the hardwood.

"Wait here," I whispered to Destiny. Then I took a brass urn and hurled it, catching the second guy in the head. I leaped from behind the table and screamed, "Get out!" at the top of my lungs, rushing up to him and kicking him in the stomach. Deacon was fighting the second guy as if it was a title match. The bad guys fought back, blow for blow, but Deacon definitely wore them down, and I was hurling anything I could at their faces. Eventually they backed out the door and ran to their car. Deacon and I decided not to give chase, and instead came over to Destiny.

"You okay?"

She nodded, and I picked her up and handed her

to Deacon so he could hold her tight and calm her. He shushed her and rocked her gentle as a teddy bear. I remembered when he used to do that for me.

"Crystal?" I looked at Deacon in a panic and went running up the staircase.

I prayed she was cowering in my bedroom, though I couldn't imagine her giving up Destiny without a fight. I went to my room and pushed open the door.

She was in my bedroom, all right. With a tourniquet around her arm and a needle hanging out, her big blue-green eyes staring straight up at the ceiling.

Rob looked at me as I finished telling him everything that happened. "You know, I could have dated a schoolteacher, a nurse, a librarian. Someone with a nice, quiet profession. But no, you have to be involved with the most crooked sport on the planet."

"Deacon and I aren't crooked."

"No. But my guess is after tonight, you're both as good as dead."

Chapter 2

Rob called 911, and while we waited, we got our stories straight. Yes, Destiny had been at the house that afternoon, but she wasn't there now. Perhaps they should begin their search with Tony Perrone.

"See," I said to Rob. "Tony has the money to pursue custody. Crystal never named Destiny's father, so he's the closest thing she's got to one. But, on the other hand, he may be the one who murdered Crystal."

"Now, wait a minute. She's got a bag of heroin up there and a needle hanging from her arm. Those two guys may have been up to no good, but they didn't murder her."

"Don't you watch *Law and Order, CSI?*"

"No. I have too much to do keeping track of my fiancée to watch TV."

"Girlfriend."

"Fiancée. You accepted the ring. It's just a long engagement, given we don't want a wedding at the state penitentiary."

"No. He has to walk me down a *real* aisle."

"Fine. Let's just call you my girlfriend for the moment, okay? So what are you saying? That they *forced* her to do heroin? Come on, Jack. This was just a bad scene all around."

I poked Rob in the chest. "Listen, Crystal didn't use drugs." I felt a choked-off sob rising in my throat at the use of the past tense when referring to her.

"I'm not trying to denigrate your friend. But when was the last time you saw her?"

"Today."

"No, before that."

"It's been a couple of years. But we spoke on the phone often."

"She was living the high life in that mansion. You don't know whether or not she was also living the *high* life. She could have been a user and you didn't know about it."

I crossed my arms. "Not Crystal. She never even smoked pot. Nothing. She was chicken. In high school, she knew this guy who smoked a joint laced with PCP and he went crazy. And she just never tried drugs. It was totally not her, Rob. Besides…I…I

stared at her there on that bed, on *my* bed. I put a…"
Suddenly, what I had been through caught up with
me, and I felt the tears starting to come, so I willed
them away. "I put a blanket on her. I couldn't bear
to see her there. Cold. And one thing I didn't see?
Track marks. Her arms were as porcelain and beautiful as the rest of her. Unmarked."

Rob looked at me, then ran upstairs. When he
came back down, he said, "I'm not sure what kind
of mess you're in, but you're right about her arms."

We heard the sirens approaching.

"Rob, when I solve her murder, I will get even
with whoever did this to her. And if I'm right, I think
all paths will lead to that snake, Benny Bonita."

"Look, this isn't Nancy Drew, Jack. Let me handle this. You worry about Destiny. Poor kid. Do you
know what, if anything, she saw?"

"No. She's shaken up, and she knows her mother's dead. But at that age…I don't know if she gets
that it means Crystal's never coming back."

"Okay, I'm giving this a day or two, tops. At some
point, you're going to have to give up Destiny. We
have to talk to her. We have to get her seen by a child
psychiatrist. Have to find out who her legal guardian
is."

"And if it's Tony Perrone, I can tell you, you're
getting her over my dead body. And I mean it. You'll
have to kill me to get her."

"You're always saying 'You'll have to kill me
first to get me to marry you without my father there,'

'You'll have to kill me first to get me to meet your parents.' One of these days, Jack, I'm going to take you up on that offer!"

"The vein in your temple is pulsing."

"Shut up!"

We heard several car doors being slammed, and suddenly my house was overrun with police and two guys from the medical examiner's office.

"Detective Carson?" Another detective, this one in a cheesy gray jacket with stains on the lapels, reeking of cologne, approached us.

"Yeah," Rob said, and stuck out his hand.

"I'm Louie Palmer. How is it you came to arrive first at the scene?"

"I'm Rob's fiancée, Jacqueline Rooney," I said. Rob shot me a look. I knew what he was thinking. *Sure, now that you need to get in good with the cops, I'm your fiancé.*

"Nice to meet you." Detective Palmer shook my hand. "You live here?"

"Correct."

He looked around the foyer at the hurled brass urn, the broken lamp, the bullet holes in the wall, the turned-over coffee table in the den, visible through the archway. "You came home to two unidentified men."

"Yes."

"And you were alone?"

I nodded.

"And you surprised them, as I understand it, according to the call Detective Carson placed."

"Yes."

"And you—" he gazed down at me "—managed to overpower and chase away a man with a semiautomatic weapon and his accomplice."

"Yes, that's precisely what I am saying."

"I'm not sure I buy that."

"I'm a trainer. Boxing. They wouldn't be the first two men I've decked."

Palmer looked at Rob, who nodded. "Trust her on that one. You don't want to cross her. On our second date, a drunk was harassing this waitress. When Jack here butted in and told him to quit it, the guy grabbed her arm. Jack broke his nose."

"I see," Palmer said. "Must make for an interesting relationship."

Rob nodded. "You don't know the half of it."

"And the woman upstairs is?"

"Crystal Lake." I saw him react to her name. "She had it legally changed to that when she moved here years ago. I only knew her by that name, and I have no idea what her given name was."

"And she's a friend of yours?"

"Old friend. Yes. I hadn't seen her in a while. She lives with Tony Perrone. She's technically his fiancée. It's his rock she's wearing on her left hand. She's the star of the Majestic show."

Palmer wiped his brow. "Tony Perrone? Jesus H. Christ, this is going to be a long night."

For the next three hours, I went over and over my story so much that *I* started to believe it. I had surprised the two men. But no, I hadn't seen Crystal's little girl. I left Deacon out of the entire equation.

Somewhere near four o'clock in the morning, the last of the police left, taking Crystal's body with them. They told me they'd like me to look at mug shots in the next day or so. Rob and I were the only ones remaining in the house.

"I need a tequila," I told him.

"You and me both."

We sat in the kitchen, and I poured us two, neat. "Screw the lemon," I said, and tossed mine back.

He slammed his back, as well. Rob has dark brown hair cut neatly and those unfathomable gray eyes of his. Sometimes at night, in bed, I had the feeling they glowed in the dark, they were so pale in the moonlight.

"I won't ever sleep in that bed again. I'm going to replace it. I don't even know if I can sleep in that room again. She didn't deserve that. And I know it has to do with the fight. With Keenan. With me and Deacon and my father."

"But you don't know that, Jack. Maybe it has to do with drugs, or with an affair she was having behind Perrone's back. Listen, as a detective, we're really a lot like archeologists. They go on a dig, and then they sift through sand, looking for tiny bone fragments—"

"You watch too much of the Discovery Channel."

"You have ADD. Let me finish. As detectives, we do the same thing. We sift through pieces of a person's life. What they've left behind. And eventually, we find the fragments we need to figure it all out. Crystal left behind all the clues we'll need. What am I saying? All the clues *I'll* need. You keep out of it."

Near dawn, just as the sun was rising, I kissed Rob goodbye, promising to talk to him later, and packed a suitcase, also grabbing Crystal's things, which I had hidden from the police. After making sure Crystal's Ferrari was still safe in the garage, and then setting the alarm for the house, I got in my car to drive to the ranch. My car is an old—I prefer "classic"—Cadillac my father had gotten for free when he and Uncle Deacon did their commercials. It was still in beautiful condition, and she was my most prized possession.

I was beyond exhausted as I headed out the highway to the ranch. Few cars were on the road, and I turned on the radio. Crystal's death was the lead story, in the true fashion of news—if it bleeds it leads. I turned off the radio, not wanting to hear it. I tried to remember the first time I met Crystal. She was the ring card girl, the woman in a bikini who walked around the boxing ring, holding a big placard pronouncing what round it was. She and I hit it off, and we became fast friends.

I looked in my rearview mirror and squinted. A shiny black car with no front license plate was a respectable distance back from me, but if I switched lanes, it switched lanes. If I sped up, it sped up.

"Christ," I muttered. I thought I should ignore it,

but I didn't want whoever it was to follow me all the way to the ranch. If I suddenly sped up, they'd know I'd spotted them. I decided I didn't care. I'd give them a run for their money.

Years before, my father's Cadillac had needed a new transmission. My father got some great idea that he'd soup up the engine a bit, too, at the same time it was at the mechanic's. So I knew my car would hold up on open road. I floored it, watching the speedometer hit 120. Luckily for me, I think the national speed limit should be about 90, anyway, and I was used to letting her fly. I headed down the flat expanse of highway, looking in my rearview mirror to see what the black car would do.

Sure enough, it was gaining on me, riding dangerously close to my bumper. Just like the evil scum who had killed Crystal and tried to take Destiny, the two guys inside looked massive and mean. They wore dark sunglasses. If I didn't know any better, I'd swear they were federal agents. But I *did* know better. They worked for either Perrone or Bonita, and my money was riding on Perrone.

I gunned the car harder, taking it to speed limits not even registering on the speedometer. I prayed the desert highways would stay empty and that I wouldn't get into an accident. At that speed, my adrenaline was causing my heart to race. I was tired, very tired, and I needed to stay on top of my game to get away from these two creeps. They nudged still closer, and taking a chance, I drove a little faster, and then spun my wheel. With a screech, I left the highway and drove into the desert, doing a tight 180-degree turn, the steering wheel fighting against me all the way on the shifting sand and pebbles, and then I drove back on the highway again.

They were still with me. I spotted a cactus up ahead. One of those big, tall Joshua trees, right out of an old Western movie set. I aimed straight toward it, as if I was playing a massive game of chicken with a twenty-foot-tall cactus. The guys in back of me followed right behind. As I left the road again, my tires spun, then I lifted my hands, as if I'd panicked, and let the car fishtail a bit. I let them think I was going to plow right into the cactus—an out-of-control female driver. But at the last minute, I grabbed the wheel and took a sharp left. Then I screamed with delight as I watched them smash their black BMW into the cactus, exploding the air bags and wrecking their car.

"Sayonara, boys," I sang, then drove steadily down the road to the ranch, the sign over the long, sandy drive proclaiming Rooney Training Camp.

Chapter 3

The first time I met Terry Keenan, I was punching a heavy bag in my uncle Deacon's gym—which was technically half my father's, though we'd transferred the title to me to avoid anyone trying to come after it to pay legal bills.

"I'm looking for Jack Rooney," he had said, surveying the gym full of fighters. The scent of stale gym socks and sweat permeated the air. I'd grown up in the stench of windowless gyms, and I was used to it after all this time.

I stopped punching the bag and turned to face him, out of breath, my arms aching slightly. I clumsily pulled the mouth guard out from between my teeth. "You're…looking…at her. My name's Jacqueline, but everyone calls me Jack."

Keenan's blue eyes narrowed. "Son of a bitch! No one told me you were a girl."

"Woman," I corrected him, less winded. "Wouldn't be the first time someone set up a fighter like that as a joke. Miguel Jimenez came looking for a guy, too."

"Well, I sure as hell am *not* training with a woman," Keenan seethed. He stood about six foot two and was in superb shape, from what I could tell as he crossed his arms across his chest, his T-shirt sleeves bulging at the biceps.

"Suit yourself," I snapped, and turned back to what I was doing, punching the bag more forcefully. As he walked away, I muttered under my breath, "Fine, asshole, don't train here, then. You and that pretty face of yours will soon regret it."

And regret it he did. Terry Keenan was back three months later, his beautiful face—big blue eyes, two dimples, a solid chin and a smattering of boyish freckles across his nose—now just a *tad* less beautiful since his nose had gotten broken, twice.

And that was how Terry Keenan came to train with me and Uncle Deacon, and now we were poised for the biggest fight of all our lives—the heavyweight championship of the world in four weeks.

"Get off the ropes!" I screamed at Terry. I looked at my uncle. "Can you see what happens when he gets backed up against the ropes like that?"

Deacon and I were standing on the ground, looking into our boxing ring, where our best chance at a title was sparring with a fighter by the name of Rock Morrison. Deacon had his arms folded, his face stony as he studied our two boxers. Deacon wasn't a screamer. I was. I would yell from the corner or scream "fake left," "jab right" or even a desperate "just fucking hit him!" Deacon, as befitted his nickname, which implied a near-biblical wisdom in the ring, studied fighters and videos of matches, and taped sparring sessions, poring over them time and time again until it became clear what our boxer was doing wrong. Then he made a pronouncement, like Moses coming down off the mount with two tablets of stone.

"All right, guys," I shouted at the fighters. "Break it up. Catch your breath."

Deacon finally spoke. "Son…" He motioned to Terry Keenan, wanting him to come closer to the ropes.

"Mmph," our fighter responded, his mouth guard still in place. He walked to us and leaned over the ropes, sweat dripping down his face.

"The good Lord gave you two legs, Terry. Both of them work just fine. But you're always relying on just one. Change up your footwork." End of pronouncement. Deacon was done for the afternoon.

"Terry, you heard him," I said. "Work out with the jump rope and then shower up. We'll look over some tapes tonight before dinner."

Terry nodded at me. That pretty face was unusual for a boxer, and his upcoming opponent, Gentleman Jake Johnson—whose face was decidedly less pretty—had offered to permanently make Terry's face ugly in all the prefight trash talking. Now Deacon and I both, privately, wondered if Keenan had also gotten another kind of offer—to take a dive. Benny Bonita couldn't be trusted, and though we believed in Terry, he had an enormous family. His seven brothers—and one sister—all seemed to think Terry was the ticket to the big time. We wondered if that meant that an even bigger paycheck, courtesy of a bribe from Bonita, was awfully enticing.

Deacon and I headed out of the gym and over to the ranch house, walking over sand and passing small cacti and scrubby-looking bushes. The ranch house was a rambling building with ten bedrooms. It had been a brothel once, and after that, it had been an actual ranch of some sort. I think the former owner had gone from hustling hookers to rustling ostriches.

I opened the front door and went into the large den, where Destiny sat watching a show with a bright purple dinosaur.

"Hi, Destiny," I said, sitting next to her and reaching out to brush a stray hair from her face.

"Hi, Auntie Jack."

"How are you doing, kiddo?" Dumb question. How was she supposed to be doing? Her mother was dead, and she was stuck with me and Deacon at a boxing camp while we figured out what to do.

"Okay. Uncle Deacon says Mommy went up to heaven." She said it very matter-of-fact. Deacon said children didn't grasp the permanence of death until ten or eleven.

"Yeah…Mommy is in heaven, sweetie pie, which is really sad. But you know what?"

"What?"

"You get to have a guardian angel. Honey, she is going to watch over you."

Destiny leaned into me, burying her face near my belly. I'd never spent much time with kids. In fact, though I felt badly for her, inside I was realizing the enormity of hiding her. I expected at any moment a phalanx of cops and FBI agents to come swooping down to grab her—and I would get a nice cell to match my father's.

"Destiny, honey…do you miss Tony?"

"Uncle Tony? Kinda. Did he go up to heaven, too?"

"No." Though I suppose to some people, Vegas is kind of like heaven. "He's back at your house."

"Did you know I have a pet tiger at our house? I couldn't pet him, but Uncle Tony let me name him."

"What'd you name him?"

"Tigger."

"Cute."

"He's *huge*. As big as one in the jungle. Uncle Tony told me he could eat me in one big gulp."

"Probably could. Did you spend a lot of time with Uncle Tony?"

She shrugged her tiny shoulders and shook her head. "Uh-uh. He was always very busy, Mommy said. I wasn't s'posed to bother him. But sometimes the three of us did stuff together. Or Mommy would take me to his work to visit him."

"Did you like visiting him at work?"

"Kinda. I drew pictures on paper in his office, and then the three of us would go out for dinner."

"What's your favorite dinner?"

"Chicken nuggets."

"I think I know how to make them," I said without enthusiasm. "But Big Jimmy does the cooking out here. I'll ask him if he can make you some."

"Big Jimmy and I made cookies."

"Really?" I knew he was a softie.

"Uh-huh. He used to be Mommy's boyfriend. She always talked about him."

"She talked about him? I didn't know that." I thought about how Crystal left Big Jimmy. She wanted the lights of Vegas to shine on her, and Big Jimmy wasn't part of that scene. If she hadn't left Big Jimmy, she'd be alive and holding Destiny instead of me.

The phone rang. I leaned over to the end table and picked it up.

"Hello?"

"Jack, it's me."

"Hi, Rob."

"Listen…Babe, what I'm hearing…the syringe… it had a fingerprint on it. Not Crystal's."

"How long can I keep hiding you know what?" I looked down at Destiny.

"I'm not sure. Not long. But for now, keep that kid safe, while I figure it out."

I stroked Destiny's cheek. "Like I said, you'd have to kill me first, Rob."

"That's exactly what I'm afraid of."

Chapter 4

Benny Bonita made Don King look modest. And, quite frankly, he made Don King look like he had a better hairdresser.

However, expensive, flashy suits and ugly pompadour aside, the reason I hated Benny Bonita was he had worn a wire two years ago in a sting that made it appear as if my father was taking a bribe to have one of his fighters throw a match. But my father wasn't doing anything of the sort. My father was trying to catch Bonita in his little scheme. It was just Dad's unfortunate luck that he had a cop named Conrad Spiller on his side—a drunken oaf he played poker with who screwed up the entire matter. And

Benny Bonita had the chief of police on his side—a slick son of a bitch named Lawrence Dillard. Which meant Dad got busted and Conrad got a desk assignment prior to early retirement, and I got broke hiring attorneys. It also meant I hated Benny Bonita with every fiber of my being.

And that evening, about an hour after I tucked Destiny in bed, Benny decided to show up at the ranch. With five bodyguards.

Perhaps *bodyguards* isn't the right term. Donald Trump has bodyguards. Dumb blond pop stars have bodyguards. Benny Bonita had five linebackers who served hard time in prison. At least that's how they looked. And they didn't ring the doorbell like the Avon lady. They sped up to the ranch in two black Hummers and almost drove through the front door.

Deacon, Big Jimmy, Miguel, Terry and Eddie the Geek, another of our trainers who insisted on wearing glasses like Buddy Holly, hence his nickname, were sitting in the den watching a TiVo'd episode of *All My Children*. Don't ask. Deacon got all the guys hooked on it years ago. He has a thing for Susan Lucci. Now they *all* have a thing for Susan Lucci.

"Good Lord Almighty! What was that?" Deacon jumped up, hearing the Hummers crash into a fence.

I raced to the front of the house and peered out a window. We had security lights that were activated when someone drove up the driveway, so the front of the house was lit up like the Vegas strip. "It looks like Bonita and several of his choirboys."

Deacon, Big Jimmy and the rest of them joined me in the foyer. Big Jimmy was packing a gun of some sort he always wore strapped to his ankle. Deacon opened the front hall closet and pulled out a rifle, and I looked for something big and heavy to beat someone over the head with—should it become necessary. And with Bonita, there was a good chance of that. I settled on a nine iron out of Deacon's golf bag.

"Not my lucky nine iron!" he shouted at me. "Are you crazy, girl? Grab the wood club."

I traded out the nine iron, and Terry and Miguel adopted fighter stances. Eddie the Geek, all five foot two of him, opened the door cautiously. Benny and his goons strode in like they owned the place.

"Well, look what the cat dragged in. Six oil-slicked rats." I sneered at them.

Bonita turned to face me. He had pockmarked skin and wore his trademark black Ray•Bans so I couldn't see beady little eyes. "Jack…Jack…still a little girl in a man's game. Haven't you learned your lesson yet, like your dear old dad?"

I raised the golf club and considered just slicing at his knees. I wanted to see him fall to the ground and beg for mercy. Deacon raised his rifle and pointed it right at Bonita's chest, causing the well-built bodyguards to all draw their weapons out from beneath their suit jackets.

"Looks like we have an old-fashioned standoff, Bonita. So why don't you and your boys get lost?" Deacon said.

"I've come for something that's mine, and I ain't leavin' till I get it."

"Not a chance," I snarled. I just wanted him to give me an excuse to club him. At that moment, I had never hated another human being so much in my life. I had visions of Crystal sprawled on my bed.

Terry Keenan was the voice of reason, coming to stand between Bonita's thugs and Deacon and me. "Come on, fellas…Jack. Let's leave the fightin' for the ring. Everybody put away your weapons." He stretched out his arms and looked from one to the other, urging calm with his steady blue gaze.

Slowly, Deacon lowered the rifle. Bonita nodded almost imperceptibly at his guys, and they reholstered their weapons. I lowered the golf club—only slightly.

Bonita's voice was gravelly. "Now, look, sweetie, your friend Crystal took something that wasn't hers to take. And I just want it back."

I was completely confused. He obviously hadn't come looking for Destiny, then. What had Crystal taken? Money? Drugs? I had to keep an advantage over him by pretending I knew what he was talking about.

"You'll get your…stuff…back when I have assurance that Destiny will be left alone. I'm not having her raised by Tony Perrone."

"You think he wants that brat? This is a lot bigger than your pretty little head can understand. You have no idea who you're messing with."

"In fact, I do. A lying, cheating snake." I walked closer to Bonita, and raised myself to my full height to stare him in the eyes—or at least in the Ray•Bans. I could smell faint garlic on his breath.

"I'm only an honest fight promoter."

"Spare me your sarcasm."

"Look, it's an ugly business, Jack. And it's no place for a lady."

"You referring to me or Crystal?"

"Both," he snarled.

That's when I'd had enough. I punched Bonita in his soft belly as hard as I could, twisting my fist upward and making sure I landed in the vicinity of his diaphragm, knocking the breath out of him. Bonita was a fight *promoter.* And unlike my father and uncle, he really wasn't a fighter—not a very good one at least, even in his prime. And he was soft. Too many women, too much booze and cigars and good casino buffets. Too much time surrounded by big burly guards who did his dirty work so he didn't have to do it himself. Just had to give the order.

Quick as lightning, he reached out a fist and grabbed hold of my hair, pulling me close to him. "Wouldn't bother me one bit to watch you die. You're just another Rooney in my way."

He released me and shoved me toward my uncle. Deacon wrapped a protective arm around me. "Vengeance is mine, sayeth the Lord."

"Yeah." I glared defiantly at Bonita. "What my uncle is saying is you'll get yours, Bonita."

"Maybe." He shrugged and signaled to his guys to leave. "But chances are you won't be around to see it."

"Don't count on it."

His bodyguards closed ranks around him, and they headed out the door. "Remember, Jack…" Bonita gave one last glance in my direction. "I want what's mine."

With that he shut the door, leaving me confused—about what he wanted—and worried. It hadn't gotten past me that Terry Keenan was the one to step between Bonita and me. I wondered whether that was out of concern for me and Deacon or a secret new loyalty to Benny Bonita.

"Is nothing sacred?" Deacon asked. "Comes to a man's home in the middle of *All My Children,* interrupting a man's private time to relax." Switching gears, he said, "I wonder what Crystal took."

I shook my head. "I don't know. Deacon, can I have a word with you?"

He nodded at the rest of them. "You all go and rewind to where we left off. And Eddie, how's about you reheat some of that jambalaya from supper? I'll be joining you in a moment."

Deacon followed me down the long hallway to the office. Walking in always filled me with a swarming sense of sentiment. I once told myself it felt as if a beehive had taken residence in my belly. While Deacon and I both had boxing memorabilia in the house, the office here at the ranch was where pictures of my life played out in living color—albeit some of that living color including putrid shades of tie-dye overdose in the outfits my father and Deacon wore in the sixties. There were pictures of the two of them as champs. But once I arrived on the scene, there were pictures of the two of them with me in diapers, with me the first time they took me fishing. Always, in every shot, Deacon was on my right and my father on my left. It was as if I had two proud fathers—and two overbearing ones the first time I went out on a date. Other pictures were of them the day they bought the gym, and then this camp. They were so proud. They had come up from nothing, two boys from a poor family in rural California. Then their father had dragged them into Los Angeles while their father and mother had struggled to find work. Deacon and Dad had dodged bullets on their way to school. And it wasn't much better in the projects at night.

Like many boxers, they had turned to the sport as a possible way out of the projects. Both brothers urged each other on. They were inseparable. And they both made it big and eventually relocated to Vegas. I was so proud of the two of them. The office was a shrine to all they had achieved—including raising me.

"Deacon…why did Terry intervene?"

"He didn't want to see anyone hurt."

"It could also be because he's on Bonita's side."

"I don't think so, Jack. Not Terry. He's worked too hard to get to this place. To have a shot at the title."

"And no one's ever thrown a title match before?" Deacon sighed.

"Would you have, Deacon? If the price was right?"

"Never. Your name is all you have in this world. You can be stripped of your possessions, even sent to prison, but an honest man has his name, his reputation. And I had a reputation as a fighter. I could walk proud."

"What about Terry, though? All those brothers and sisters looking for a handout. They call here with their problems—can I borrow a thousand for a down payment on a new car, my kid needs braces. Whatever. One even called begging for money so he could start this 'sure thing' business selling water filters or something. Multilevel marketing. A scam."

"Yeah, but remember when Terry came back? He wanted to win so badly he could taste it."

Terry had swallowed a lot of pride to come back and train with Deacon and me. As it was, a lot of people in the fight biz assumed once my father got sent to prison, the Rooney fighters would leave in droves. After all, they were used to training with two champions. Not one champion and one *girl.* Terry had walked out just at the sight of me. But when he came back to the Rooney camp, he was willing to train with a girl, willing to do *anything* to win.

"Maybe you're right, Deacon. I don't know. Since Miguel lost so badly, since Crystal, I'm paranoid as hell."

"Me, too," he said quietly. "How's Baby Girl?" He had taken to calling Destiny that.

I shrugged. "How could she be doing? Her mother was murdered, she's sent out to the desert to a camp with a bunch of virtual strangers. She's suffering, the poor thing."

"You know sooner or later Rob's going to come out here with an order to take her. If we're *lucky,* he'll be able to do it without all of us getting arrested."

I looked on the wall at a picture of me when I was Destiny's age. Maybe I had grown up in gyms that reeked of sweat, watching men try to beat each other up, but it was an idyllic childhood in many ways. I had always known I was loved.

"I'm going to check on her." I kissed Deacon on the cheek and left the office and walked down the long hall to the bedroom Destiny and I shared. We had decided after her trauma, it would be best if she could look over and see me there next to her at night.

The light was on. She insisted on it, and I sure as hell wasn't going to argue with her after all she had been through. The TV was on, too, "for company." She was watching the *Wiggles* video, which was her favorite. She watched it over and over and over again. I was getting rather sick of *The Wiggles.* Five men in asexual turtlenecks singing songs and prancing about with an octopus. Kind of weird.

She was still awake.

"Hey there, sweetie pie. Can't sleep?"

She shook her head.

I sat next to her and stroked her cheek. "I know things are really scary right now. Really confusing. But I promise you I'm going to take care of you. Do you know that, at least?"

She nodded. "My mommy said you were her best friend. You and Big Jimmy were her two favorite people in the world—except for me. I was her favoritest favorite."

I smiled. "What about Tony? Wasn't he one of her favorites?"

She scrunched up her face. "She said it was complicated."

"Yeah, well, with grown-ups, sometimes life is pretty complicated."

"I saw him, you know."

"Who, honey?"

"That bad man. Tonight. I heard the crash, and then I looked out the window. I saw him and hid under the bed."

"Benny Bonita?"

She nodded, wide-eyed.

"Don't worry, he's gone."

"I know," she whispered. "He scared my mommy."

"How do you know that?"

"She said so."

I slid down so that I was lying next to her on the king-size bed. "You know, let's not think about all this right now. Let's get some sleep, okay?"

"Can we say prayers?"

My father was steadfastly agnostic. Deacon filled my head with the Lord this and the Lord that. And as for me, praying wasn't my strong suit. "Sure kid. You have one in mind?"

"No. I just say God bless Mommy. And God bless Big Jimmy. And God bless Auntie Jack. And God bless Uncle Deacon. Amen. Oh, yeah. And, God? Please make Mr. Bonita stay far, far away."

"I'll say amen to that," I whispered, and held her hand until she fell asleep.

Chapter 5

The next morning, early, Destiny woke me up. I groaned. "Kid…it's way too early to get up. Why don't you watch those wiggle-worm guys."

She giggled. *The Wiggles.*

"Yeah. Them." I rolled over and pulled the covers over my head.

"I'm hungry."

"Go get yourself something to eat," I said from under the covers.

"Like what?"

"Deacon will make you a smoothie."

"He makes gross ones."

"There's leftover jambalaya in the fridge."

"Yuck. For breakfast?"

"I've been eating cold leftovers for breakfast since before you were born. They're good for you."

"Breakfast is s'posed to be something like cereal or pancakes."

"That's a conspiracy dreamed up by Mr. Kellogg and Mr. Post."

"You're not very good at baby-sitting," she said.

So the little pip-squeak guilted me into getting up. I pulled on a robe and shuffled out to the kitchen where Deacon—who always rises before dawn—was sipping a smoothie the color of what the devil spewed in *The Exorcist*. It was enough to make me gag.

"Hello, Baby Girl." Deacon smiled at Destiny.

"Hello, not-so-baby girl." He looked up at me.

"Don't press your luck," I snapped. "The kid here wants breakfast food. Pancakes or cereal."

"How about eggs?" Deacon smiled at her again. I remembered that smile. He was always smiling at me when I was little, seemingly delighted just to be around me.

"I don't like eggs."

"Pancakes it is, then."

Deacon rose from his chair and started opening up cabinets, looking for Bisquick and syrup. As he puttered, the doorbell rang. Deacon and I exchanged glances.

"I'll get it," Deacon said grimly. The ranch was far enough off the beaten path that no one showed up there unless he or she was really looking for us—good or bad.

I immediately pulled Destiny over on my lap and eyed the butcher block full of knives that was two feet from us on the counter. I'd never let anyone take her without a fight.

I listened for sounds of a scuffle, but didn't hear any.

"Look who," Deacon said, coming back a minute or so later with Rob in tow.

"Rob!" I gave Destiny a hug, then slid her off my lap and jumped up to give Rob a bear hug. "God, is it good to see you."

"This beats the 'No, I'm not going to marry you yet' greeting." He hugged me back, and as usual, I could feel his chest against mine, solid and absolutely rock hard.

"Well, I can tell you we're not getting married in the midst of all this chaos."

"Believe it or not, I'm with you on that. This case gets weirder and weirder." He looked over at Destiny and then walked over to the table where she sat. I don't even know if she recognized him from the night her mother was killed. I was amazed at her resilience so far, but that night, she had to have been in shock. Deacon said her teeth had chattered for four straight hours after he got her to the ranch. Then she'd passed out, exhausted.

Rob knelt in front of her, I assumed to make himself less imposing. "Hi, Destiny. I'm Jack's friend,

Rob. I'm a policeman, and I catch bad guys. And I'm going to make sure nothing happens to you or Jack, okay?"

She nodded. Rob tousled her hair.

Deacon opened a cabinet door. "I was just getting ready to make Baby Girl pancakes. It's good to have a child around this old ranch again."

"Pancakes? You like pancakes?" Rob looked at Destiny. She nodded again. "You sure you wouldn't rather have toasted spider legs?"

I watched Destiny stifle a giggle. She shook her head.

"What about fried cactus?"

She shook her head again, her eyes twinkling just a tiny bit.

"How about sautéed monkey feet?"

"Gross!" she said, laughing.

"Well—" Rob put on a disappointed face "—if I can't talk you into any of those delicacies, could I make you my special German pancakes? It's a recipe from my great-grandmother on my mother's side, and be prepared to never want any other kind of pancake for the rest of your life!"

I loved watching the gentleness in his face. I had seen him, more than a few times, break up a bar fight or come to the aid of someone on the street, even when he was off duty. He was always supremely calm and competent. Sometimes, like when this one guy in a bar had grabbed his cocktail waitress by the hair and threatened her, Rob's eyes went stormy and you knew he wasn't a person to trifle with. But he and I had never discussed children. Maybe it was because I had spent my life immersed in a world of men, always trying to prove I was as tough as the guys. Maybe he didn't think I was the "mommy" type. But he sure was the daddy type.

Rob commandeered the kitchen. Next thing I knew, at the picnic-style long table that served as our kitchen table, Big Jimmy, Miguel, Terry and a couple of other sparring partners and trainers, and little Destiny, were chowing down on pancakes fried in enough oil to lube a car. The pancakes were slightly crispy, golden and beyond delicious, and Rob went through two boxes of Bisquick feeding the gang.

After everyone was sitting around groaning about how full they were, I grabbed Rob's hand and said, "Let's take a walk."

Big Jimmy looked at me and gave a slight nod. "I'll take Destiny into the den. Come on, sugar, let's go color." The sight of Big Jimmy, all three hundred pounds of muscle, long black braid down his back, scooping up Destiny like a little doll, made me smile. He was the proverbial big teddy bear.

Rob and I strolled out into the rocky yard and off toward the mountains. The air was fresh, and he held my hand.

"I've missed you, Jack."

"You're just saying that, but secretly you're glad I'm not squeezing your toothpaste tube from the middle," I said, referring to his somewhat anal-retentive neatness and my…well, my sloppiness.

"I like when you do that. The next time I go to use my toothpaste, it reminds me that you were there. It makes me hopeful that one day, you'll be there permanently."

"Rob…"

"I know." He put up his hands. "I won't bother you about it. Just know, even with all this crazy shit going on that I love you. Even though I have a feeling you may be the reason my blood pressure is a little high and this little vein here—" he pointed to his temple "—throbs with regularity."

"I'm proud of that little vein."

"You know you can't hide her forever, right?"

I nodded. "I keep expecting to see my face and an Amber Alert up on the television. What gives? Why hasn't Perrone pressured the cops to find Destiny?"

"I don't know. In fact, they've pretty much pulled me off the case. They have me working that murder over on the Strip. Because Crystal was Perrone's fiancée, and because Perrone is one of the top two hundred wealthiest men in the world, and because the chief is a friend of Perrone's from way back, this has a hands-off atmosphere about it. I was told to forget the angle she was murdered."

"What about the fingerprint?"

"They're going with it belonged to her dealer, that this is like some John Belushi case of a dealer shooting someone up and it just being too much and she died. Perrone is saying she had a drug problem. He even produced a letter from some doctor friend of his saying he treated her privately for drug abuse."

"But her arms were clear. You saw them."

"I didn't say this doesn't stink to high heaven like a bad fish, Jack. I'm just saying what the party line is."

"And Destiny?"

"Perrone's saying he wants her found privately. He says he knows where she is and it's a family matter until he says otherwise."

"And you?" I turned to look into his eyes, amazed in the sunlight at how clear and gray they were.

He clenched his jaw and glanced away. "She was your friend. I'm going to get to the bottom of it. But that doesn't mean I want you snooping around."

"Well, you better get to the bottom of it quickly because I'm not going to park myself out here like a sitting duck. Did you know Benny Bonita paid us a visit last night with a few of his posse?"

"What'd that asshole want?"

"Something that Crystal 'took' from him."

"What?"

"I have no idea."

"Did you check her suitcases?"

I looked at him. "That must be why you're the detective and I try to get men to punch each other's lights out for a living. Come on."

I jogged toward the house, and Rob tagged along behind me. Quietly, we let ourselves into the house and moved down the hall to the office. I didn't want Destiny to see us going through her mother's belongings. Deacon had hidden her luggage in a locked closet. All of them were Louis Vuitton suitcases that probably cost more than my entire wardrobe.

On top of the first suitcase was a huge makeup bag. I started with that, going through each cosmetic—and there were a lot of them. I opened each compact, each jar of wrinkle cream, each tube of cleanser, everything. I smelled each one, thinking maybe they concealed drugs. All the cosmetics and skin products were from La Prairie—one of the most expensive cosmetic companies in the world. But nothing else.

"Damn!" I looked at Rob.

"Keep searching."

We went through suitcase after suitcase, each piece of clothing.

"Feel along the hems," Rob told me. "In case she sewed something into the lining of a skirt or a pair of pants."

"Like what?"

"Like a safety deposit box key or the key to a locker. I don't think she'd really be so dumb as to have whatever it is on her."

After an hour of careful fingering of her clothes, we came up with nothing. Now that the suitcases were empty, Rob and I began moving our hands along the seams, feeling the bottoms, looking for any indication there was a secret hiding spot.

"Nothing," I said disgustedly. I looked around at the floor where all her flashy-trashy Vegas clothes lay—sequins and tight low-ride jeans, stiletto Jimmy Choos. Suddenly, I felt tears overtaking my eyes. "This is all that's left of a life, Rob. This and Destiny."

He reached out to rub my shoulders. "Baby, she touched a lot of lives. And that's always going to be with you and Deacon and Big Jimmy."

"Yeah." I wiped at my face. "And when I find out who killed her, his life isn't going to be worth shit."

"Jack..." Rob's voice was warning and measured.

"Like you said. This whole thing stinks like rotten fish. And I'm not going to let her die without a word, just swept under Tony Perrone's carpet."

"Did I ever tell you that you scare me sometimes?"

"You tell me that all the time."

"Yeah, but this time, Jack, I really mean it."

Chapter 6

Rob left in the afternoon, with a passionate kiss and a promise to continue looking into Crystal's death. I took Destiny and went over to the gym to see how training was going.

We had two full-size boxing rings out in an enormous barn. Jimenez was in one, and Keenan was in another. They were sparring with two up-and-coming boxers—one a kid from the barrio in L.A. and the other a refugee from Kosovo whose real name was unpronounceable to most of the guys, so they called him Sovo.

Big Jimmy came over to Destiny and me and picked her up. In his arms, she looked even tinier.

"Now, don't you get scared, Destiny. They're pretend fighting," he soothed.

"It looks like they're really fighting."

Gazing into the ring, I knew she was right. Sparring has a lot of heavy breathing, spitting, snorting, and the sounds of glove smacking flesh and boxing shoes shuffling on canvas, same as a real fight.

"Well, Destiny," I said. "It may look real, but in sparring, they're practicing for a real fight, and so they don't try to hurt each other quite so much. Sometimes someone has a lucky shot, of course. But mostly they're just practicing."

"Why do people fight?"

"Fight? Well, this is boxing. And it's a sport. Just two guys, two athletes, highly trained, in a ring, seeing who can outbox the other. And sometimes the two boxers don't like each other, but it's not like a real fight. I mean, there are rules and judges and even doctors standing by to stop the fight if it looks like someone's really gotten hurt."

I watched her as she stared at the men in the two rings. Every once in a while, she winced. I'd grown up in gyms. I can't recall if I ever winced, though Deacon told stories of how, when my father and he used to fight, the other brother would take me along to the match, and I would cover my eyes if they started losing. But eventually, Deacon said, I stopped covering my eyes and started yelling at the judges if they scored the fight incorrectly—or at least in a way I didn't agree with.

Big Jimmy patted her back. He was one-quarter Cherokee, and the size of a tank. His hair was jet black, almost blue, and his face, considering how many fights he'd been in, was regal with wide slashes of cheekbones and a straight—for a boxer—nose. Big Jimmy was a motorcycle-club member years before, a real hell-raiser. He drank too much, and my father told me he sold crystal meth and was just bad news. He'd been arrested for something, and he had to do some community service to get his record expunged. So he took a job helping out at my father's and Deacon's summer camp, working with underprivileged kids. From that experience, he got in the ring and began channeling his anger and energies into fights. He did pretty well, too, until he tore his rotator cuff. That's when they offered to make him their cornerman. He had great instincts in the ring. And he was the best cornerman in the business.

He became part of our inner circle. And then, when we all met Crystal that night she was a ring card girl, he was a goner. He really loved her. He brought her flowers, he held open doors, and she told me that in the bedroom, he rocked her world. But no one ever gets wealthy being a cornerman. Hell, not many people get wealthy training fighters. It was my uncle Deacon's investments that fed his lifestyle. Of course, now that Terry had a real title shot, we all stood to make some serious money.

I concentrated on Terry for a while, yelling instructions from ringside. "Dance more. You're planting your feet too much. Stop dropping that left shoulder and telegraphing your left hook…jab…jab…work on the body, tire him out."

Destiny and Big Jimmy came over to ringside, too.

"What are you telling them?" she asked.

"You ever study spelling words or anything in school?"

"Sometimes."

"Well, you study words to learn how to spell. I study boxing films to make Terry a better boxer."

"What do you mean? Like you go to the movies?"

"Kind of. Now, the best boxer who ever lived, probably, was Muhammad Ali. Graziano, now he had a punch that could knock a man from here to Kansas. But Ali was the whole package—footwork, strong punch, tireless, and with so much charisma, honey, he could light up a room. And do you know what he called himself? What his nickname was?"

"No."

"The Greatest. As in the greatest fighter…ever."

"Wow!"

"Right. So back in the den, we have hundreds of videos of fights and matches, of the most brutal, most grueling fights, of the fights that were over in twenty-seven seconds…"

"Twenty-seven seconds?"

"Yeah. There was a time when Iron Mike Tyson had the world fooled that he was invincible. And he took down everybody with these shots that just—

boom—brought them down quickly. So we study him. We study all of them. And then we have to figure out what Terry and Miguel are doing wrong and what they're doing right. And we build on that."

"I don't think I'd want to be a boxer. It would hurt."

"Yeah, well, sometimes it does hurt."

I looked at her and memories flooded back of the first time I saw my father badly beaten.

"Hey, Princess," he whispered, his voice barely a rasp. He was in a hospital bed, and Uncle Deacon used his status as reigning champ to bend the hospital rules so that I could go to my father's bedside. I was seven years old.

"Oh, Daddy." I rushed over to him and flung my head on his belly and hugged him. He winced.

"You probably shouldn't hug Daddy right now," Deacon said, coming over to me and patting my back.

I lifted my head and took a small step backward, tears blurring my vision. "You look terrible, Daddy." His head was bandaged where he had sustained a deep gash over his left eye. He had a concussion. His face was swollen and bruised. It almost wasn't recognizable as a human face in spots. Oxygen tubes were inserted in his nose, and he had two different IV lines flowing into his veins.

"They should have stopped the fight sooner," Deacon said, worry reflected in his eyes.

"Nah. I wanted to keep going."

"Then it's time to retire."

"I'm what? Thirty-three? And it's over? What? Boxers live in dog years?"

His hands were swollen, the knuckles arthritic already. I bent my head and kissed one.

"You know they live in dog years, Sean," Deacon said. "One year in the ring is like seven out in the real world. You can't keep going."

"Please, Daddy. Listen to Uncle Deacon."

"Don't worry about me, Princess. Your old man will be okay." My shoulders shook as I tried to be tough and hide my tears.

Deacon leaned down and told me, "Hush, Jackie, hush. Your daddy's going to be just fine. Lord, did I ever tell you about my fight with Chi-Chi Valasquez?"

I shook my head, not wanting to hear another fight story. The sobs came harder, from a place inside my chest. Great, racking sobs. The two men, the two tough guys, looked at each other in panic. Finally, my father said, "How about if I make you a deal?"

I looked at his face. His eyes were almost swollen shut, just slits, and he had to lean his head against the pillows to try to see me through them.

"What kind of deal?" I sniffled.

"One rematch. One rematch…so I can go out on top. I'll train harder than ever before. You'll be my trainer. We'll run together. We'll punch the bag together. It'll be fun. One more rematch, and then win or lose, I'll retire."

I thought about it. I stared at his face and part of me wanted to tell him—no, beg him—to quit. Right there, right then. But I knew, even as a little girl, that fighting was in the Rooney brothers' blood. So I nodded and whispered, "Deal."

He was released two days later, and within days my father and Deacon set about turning me into a junior trainer. I learned all there was to learn about boxing, and I soaked it up, because I foolishly believed if I didn't study hard enough, if I, if *we*, didn't train hard enough, then my father would again get beaten badly. That maybe next time he'd get killed— it occasionally happened in the ring—and it would be all my fault. The pressure I felt was immense. I lived, breathed, slept and ate boxing. My room was covered in posters of fighters and covers of *Ring* magazine. I learned how to tape my father's hands before they were inserted in his gloves. I learned to lace the gloves. I carried buckets of spit and water from the corner. I swept the canvas ring. I worked myself almost to the point of exhaustion.

And he won. He won the rematch. My father went out as a champ. True to his word, he retired. Then he and Deacon opened their gym and the ranch and attracted young fighters eager to learn.

As for me, the ordeal and months of training turned me into a true Rooney. From that point on, boxing was in my blood, too.

* * *

Terry and Sovo were sparring, working on their footwork, always one of Terry's weak points. He'd gotten a lot better since training with us. Before, he had always relied on his sheer size to overwhelm opponents, but he wouldn't be able to do that with Jake Johnson, who was just an inch shorter at six foot one, and weighed in at ten pounds heavier—a good 225 pounds. Terry had always just come out swinging. He was a slugger. Now, over time, he still had a powerful punch, but we had studied enough films, sparred endlessly and brought him through several professional bouts. He was more of a true boxer.

Sovo wasn't even breathing hard. His physical shape was amazing. He was an up-and-comer. I told Deacon that the war in Sovo's country, all he had seen, gave him a hunger that, frankly, few people have. He had fought on several undercards—the lesser fights on a ticket leading up to the main event on fight night. But Deacon and I figured Sovo was our next big thing. So did a number of sportswriters. When they called to interview Deacon, they asked how Terry was, but the next question out of their mouths was always about Sovo. They called him the Kosovo Killer. Nothing like boxing for its wacky nicknames.

Sovo threw a solid right at Terry, who caught the punch full in the sternum, winding him for a second. Suddenly, Terry turned crazy. I'd never seen that look in him before, but he went after Sovo as if it was the final fight scene in the movie *Rocky.* I screamed, "Cool it, Terry," but he wasn't listening. It was as if this fury had come up inside him.

Deacon came rushing over, and we both climbed into the ring. Sovo was pissed off now, and the two of them were slugging it out.

"Break it up," I yelled, literally hurting my throat with the fierceness of my voice. I was also trying to avoid getting punched out as I pushed on Terry's back. "Stop it, Terry!"

Deacon took on Sovo. The entire gym had stopped fighting, and the men were watching us as we tried to get these two guys to back off each other. I pushed harder on Terry's back and Deacon wedged himself between the two of them, though they were still trying to get at each other.

"Guys…guys…you're brothers in this camp. In the Lord's name, I tell you to stop!" Deacon now looked like a wrestler, trying to wrap his arms around Sovo, who was slippery with sweat and had a forty-pound advantage over Deacon.

I pulled my fist back, and as hard as I could, I punched Terry in the upper arm. Suddenly, he turned on me and raised his fist, and *bam,* he slugged me in the shoulder. Hard.

I fell backward, without even breaking my fall, on the canvas, saw stars and felt a pain I had never felt before. From somewhere out in the gym, I heard Destiny scream. Now Terry seemed to come to his senses.

"Christ, what am I doing?" He seemed stunned at his own actions. He stuck a gloved hand down and helped me to my feet. My shoulder felt as if it was broken. I didn't think it was—prayed it wasn't. However, I knew if I didn't get some ice on it right away, I wouldn't be able to move it for days. I'd just sustained a knockout blow from the hopefully soon-to-be heavyweight champion of the entire world.

Sovo was breathing heavy and staring at Terry with hatred in his eyes. I knew no matter how badly my shoulder hurt, I had to diffuse their hostility toward each other.

"It happens, Sovo," I whispered, as unwanted tears involuntarily flowed down my face from the pain.

"What happens?" Sovo asked, nastily, then he let out a stream of curse words—or what I assumed were curse words—in his native tongue.

"That a sparring round gets carried away once in a while."

Terry turned to Sovo. "Man, I don't know what came over me. Please, Sovo, accept my apologies."

Deacon put an arm around Sovo's shoulders. Deacon and Sovo were close. The barrios may not be Kosovo, but they were both men who were children of war of some sort. "Now, son, I believe Terry here is offering a humble and heartfelt apology. It's only right to forgive, Sovo."

Sovo nodded. He said something under his breath,

but he punched gloves with Terry, then retreated from the ring. As soon as everyone went back to what they were doing, I nearly collapsed.

"Damn, Jack, damn," Terry said, his eyes actually moist. Something was really bothering him. Not the least of which he'd just punched his trainer—and a girl at that.

"Big Jimmy!" Deacon shouted, and they helped me out of the ring and over to Big Jimmy, whose face was dark and furious as he glared at Terry. This wasn't good. Less than four weeks out from the fight of all our lives, and our camp was in disarray, not to mention we were illegally hiding Destiny.

Big Jimmy's role in the corner of the ring in any match was to tend to cuts, bruises and rubdowns, to keep the fighter going, to remind him to breathe deeply, to dump water over his head to cool him down and to assuage, in the literally few seconds he had, gashes and swelling eyes and bloody noses. I've even seen him take a cold "iron" (at least that's what it looks like) and use it to flatten swelling eyelids. Eye injuries are some of the most dangerous, because if your eye is swelling shut, you can't see well enough to block punches. But at that precise moment in the gym, I felt like a shoulder injury was about the worst thing a man—or woman—could go through.

Big Jimmy had handed Destiny off to Eddie the Geek, who sat at a table coloring a *Wiggles* picture with her—intently. Eddie was focusing on her and smiling. She glanced over at me, and I tried to smile so she would think all was well. But really, it was more like a grimace.

The guys helped me into our medical room. We had our first aid supplies, tape, a whirlpool to soothe injuries, a long massage table and other equipment in there.

The guys helped set me down on the table.

"Take off your shirt, Jack," Big Jimmy intoned.

Christ, he'd seen me drunk, he'd seen me the time we all went skinny-dipping on the Fourth of July. I took off my top but kept my sports bra on.

"Jesus H. Christ," Big Jimmy whistled, looking at the spot where Terry's glove had landed.

I glanced down at my shoulder, which was turning shades of red and purple I didn't even realize were in the color spectrum. "Oh, my God!"

Everyone looked at Terry, who suddenly collapsed on the bench, his head in his hands.

"All right! I can't hold it in anymore. Bonita tried to bribe me. More like extortion, actually."

As Big Jimmy prepared packs of ice for my shoulder, Deacon sat next to Terry.

"I'm going to ask you one time, Terry. What in the name of God's good earth is going on?"

Terry looked up at us all as Big Jimmy fussed over my shoulder, using an Ace bandage to keep bags of ice on my shoulder.

"First of all, Jack, I'm so, so sorry. I lost my head, and I'm sick inside that I hurt you."

"You're lucky I don't take you out back and teach you a lesson," Big Jimmy snapped.

"Now, Jimmy…" Deacon tried to soothe us with his warm tone of voice.

I winced as Big Jimmy moved my shoulder. "Ain't broken," he said, and looking at Terry he added, "Lucky for you."

"All right, Terry, tell us what happened," I whispered.

"It's my brother. He was arrested for selling drugs. But it seemed like a setup. At least that's what my bro says now. Stupid idiot. I mean, if it felt like a setup, the time to stop going through with it was *before* the commando-type police raid. Jesus. And my brother's looking at a 'three strikes, you're out' kind of deal. He's looking at some real hard time. Anyway, Bonita found out and said if I threw the fight, my brother would be released on a 'technicality.' The evidence would be lost. And there was an extra million dollars in it for me if I went down."

My shoulder throbbed. "Look, Terry, I'm sorry about your brother. Hell, I'm sorry about my own father. I'm sorry about a lot of things. But you can't throw the fight. If you're in trouble, you need to come to Deacon and me, not Bonita."

"He approached *me*."

"When?"

"Few weeks ago. I was out at a club, tossing back some Cristal with a gorgeous blonde, and next thing I know, I come back to my car and five guys are leaning against it. I thought maybe I could do it. Maybe it wouldn't bother me. But I can't do it. I can't take a dive. You guys have to believe me. I'm just afraid for my family if I don't do what he wants. Not me. Hell, I can handle whatever shit Bonita sends my way, but I've got a big family and some of them are pretty messed up. They don't need more chaos in their lives."

"And that's what he's counting on. The pressure of being the breadwinner for a large family," I said. "All right. We'll have to just deal with the situation day by day. Big Jimmy?"

"Yeah."

"We're going to have to tighten up security."

"Sure thing." Big Jimmy's "security detail" was a posse of former Hell's Angels and other motorcy-cle-club members. They were guys who had eventu-ally married and settled down, had a kid or two, and weren't so concerned with raising hell anymore. However, that didn't mean they weren't up to kick-ing some ass if need be.

"Terry, until the fight is over, maybe you should ask your family to lie low," Deacon said.

"I already did. I sent two of my brothers to go stay with my sister, and I've told them all to be careful."

The ice was making my shoulder cold, but not necessarily numb. It hurt like hell. Big Jimmy came over to me with two painkillers, which I gratefully swallowed with a cup of water.

Terry's face was pale. "Jack, Big Jimmy, Deacon…I'm sorry. I should have come to you sooner. The pressure's making me crack. Jack, I never should've hit you. I don't know what came over me."

"It's over and done with," I said.

"See if you're still saying the same thing tomorrow," Big Jimmy intoned. "When your shoulder is the color of an eggplant."

"Look, it's been a long afternoon. Terry, why don't you call it a day? And Jimmy, you take Destiny and Eddie back to the house…and tell Miguel to get his ass in here."

Big Jimmy and Terry left the medical room, and a few minutes later, gloves off but tape still on his hands, Miguel Jimenez knocked on the door and came in.

"How's your shoulder, Jack?"

I pushed the ice aside to show him the bruising.

"Man, he got you damn good. What the hell was up with him in the ring?"

"Same thing, I think, as your fight the other night."

Jimenez looked away. His face, which had looked like a bunch of dark blue grapes after his defeat the other night, had faded to a yellow-green-blue bruise.

"Look at me, Miguel."

But he couldn't.

Deacon motioned toward a bench and said, "Sit down, Miguel."

Miguel did, and I could see his hands trembling a little.

"Whatever it is," Deacon said, "you can tell us."

Miguel wouldn't talk.

"Was it Bonita?" I asked.

He nodded.

"How'd he get to you? What'd he promise?"

"Green cards and jobs for my mother and sister. Some money."

"Fuck, this mess just gets deeper and nastier. Like *Alice in Wonderland,* only I went down a manhole instead of a rabbit hole and ended up in Bonita's sewer."

Miguel looked absolutely devastated. "I'm sorry, Jack. It won't ever happen again." He looked at Deacon. "You have to believe me."

"Son, we took you in. We fed you, clothed you, trained you. We've done everything we can for you, and now you don't come to us? Instead you go to *Bonita,* when Jack and I told you, specifically, what had happened to her father."

Jimenez nodded. "I know. I feel terrible."

Deacon softly said, "A viper has come into our home, our camp. Go shower. I have a lot of things to think about."

Without another word, Miguel slowly walked out into the main training area. Deacon walked over to shut the door.

"Are you going to cut him loose?" I asked.

"I don't know. I don't think so."

"He betrayed us. They both did. How can we trust them in the ring?"

"A man who, with his heart full of remorse, re-pents, deserves a second chance."

"That's bullshit."

"Bullshit or not, I've known Miguel for a long time. At heart he's a good boy."

"They're not boys, Deacon. They're men, so stop making excuses. Doesn't loyalty mean any-thing to you?"

"Of course it does. I just have a little room in my heart for forgiveness. You, on the other hand, still carry a grudge against a girl from seventh grade who stole your boyfriend."

"That's not true. The only person I carry a major grudge against is Benny Bonita."

"Well," Deacon said, coming over to me and help-ing me down from the table, ice held in place by an Ace bandage. "Can't say as I blame you one bit for that one."

We went through the gym, turning off lights, and slowly made our way to the ranch house. Though it was full of people, I felt lonelier than ever, knowing that two men I trusted had betrayed Deacon and me. I dragged the heels of my cowboy boots, dust kick-ing up as we walked.

Chapter 7

The next day my cell phone rang and woke me up. I looked in the bed next to me and remembered that Big Jimmy had come into the bedroom early to help Destiny get dressed and to repack my shoulder. He was going to take her for a drive to a friend of his with a horse farm.

"Hello?"

"It's me, Jack."

"Hi, Rob."

"That was the most monotone greeting I've ever heard. What's eating you?"

"Well, for starters, I took a solid left hook from Terry Keenan last night."

"He hit you?"

"Yeah. Didn't mean to. His emotions kind of ran away with him in the ring."

"He *hit* you?"

"Please, Rob, don't make this into some big deal when it's not."

"Jack, not too many guys could handle their fiancée working in a boxing ring to begin with, spending all her free time talking about the muscles and bodies of other men, their punches, their stances. You have to admit I'm pretty mellow when it comes to what you do for a living. But call me crazy, a guy doesn't like hearing the woman he's madly in love with—for reasons that often are unclear to him—has been punched by the future heavyweight champion of the world."

"Please, it's a little bruise."

"Sure. And you're a little stubborn."

"Anyway, Bonita has been trying to extort my guys big-time. Bribe 'em, whatever. He finds their weaknesses, in both Terry's and Miguel's case a soft spot for their families, and he exploits it."

"And you've never considered taking a job as a kindergarten teacher? Away from the cesspool that is professional boxing."

"No. And I don't ask you to stop being a cop, Rob. I don't tell you about the nights I turn on the evening news or read about a cop getting shot and wonder if you're in an E.R. somewhere bleeding to fucking death!"

"You worry about me?" He sounded surprised.

"Shut up."

"I mean it. You worry about me?"

"Of course I do, you big idiot."

"Jack Rooney does, indeed, have a soft spot. Let me alert the media."

"Next time I see you, remind me to punch you."

"No. Because I have some good news. You may want to *kiss* me."

"Yeah?"

"Crystal had a lawyer."

"What do you mean?"

"I mean a business card was found in her personal possession according to the police inventory report. A single business card. No other cards, nothing on her cell phone, no other clues. But one business card. The name and address of one Charlie Esposito, Esquire."

"And?"

"And how much money is Tony Perrone worth?"

"Zillions. I don't know. Why?"

"Because Tony Perrone's lawyer for his business and personal affairs is Jason White of White, White and Taylor. He happens to be almost as loaded as Perrone. It's one of those clubby firms. Lots of dough. They're not even listed in the phone book. 'Cause if you're looking up an attorney in the yellow pages, you can't afford these guys."

"So?"

"So, wouldn't you think that Crystal, as his fiancée, living in the lap of luxury, dropping thousands and thousands just on shoes each month, when it came time to put her affairs in order, to name a guardian for Destiny, to figure out her will, to whatever…wouldn't you think she'd go to Jason White?"

"Sort of, yeah."

"Or if not him, then some high-priced lawyer?"

"Yes. I mean, she started out not knowing the difference between cheap wine you buy at 7-Eleven, and worked her way up to knowing every French wine in Tony's cellar."

"Exactly."

I sat up, slowly. My shoulder felt as if a two-ton safe had fallen on it. I couldn't even move my arm.

"Who's this lawyer again?"

"Charlie Esposito. A lawyer who went to some Caribbean law school somewhere. And he barely scrapes by, moonlights a bit as a private eye. I don't know. All I do know is he has a rat-hole office in the worst—and I mean worst—part of town. Most of his clients are thugs and lowlifes looking to cop a plea."

I ran my hand through my hair. "Wait a minute. He's a criminal attorney?"

"Yeah. And the story I'm hearing is she went to *him* to draw up her will."

"But that makes no sense."

"I know. Now he's spouting about attorney-client privilege and the chief doesn't want anyone looking at this too hard. But something's really funny about this, Jack. What kind of car did Crystal drive?"

"This year? A Ferrari. She got a new leased car every year with Tony. Last year it was a Mercedes. Always in blue to match her eyes."

"Yeah. Well, Esposito's office is on Chance Boulevard. And if she drove there, in her car, with her looks, she was sure as hell taking a chance."

"So what do we do next?"

"*We* don't do anything. I'm going to try to do some unobtrusive police work. Remember, technically, I'm off the case."

"Okay."

"Okay? You're not going to argue with me?"

"No."

"All right, then. I'll come out to the ranch late tonight. Thought I'd spend the night."

"Okay."

"I love you, Jack."

"I love you, too."

I hung up the phone and gingerly climbed out of bed. I didn't argue with him because it would do no good. I was *going* to see Charlie Esposito. As soon as I figured out how to drive with only one arm.

Unlike Crystal's, my car fit in the very questionable neighborhood of burnt-out storefronts and cheap liquor stores that housed Charlie Esposito's office. I also drove with a crowbar on the seat next to me, and I had "borrowed" a gun of Deacon's from the office. I'm not a great shot, but I hoped whatever I faced at Esposito's office wouldn't require gunfire.

Driving with one arm wasn't that tricky—until it was time to parallel park on the street. That proved complicated—and painful. When I got out of my car, I was parked crooked and eight inches from the curb. "That'll have to do," I muttered under my breath, and then walked up to building 909.

The door to the street was made of metal, and I pushed on it and found myself in a very ill-lit hallway, with a flight of stairs leading up. Esposito's office was on the second floor. I climbed the steps and found his office, which had Charles A. Esposito, Attorney at Law typed on a piece of paper and *taped* to the door. Had to hand it to Crystal, she found herself a winner of an attorney.

I knocked. There was no answer. I knocked again more loudly. Still no answer. I looked at my watch. Eleven o'clock. A little too early for lunch. I tried the doorknob; it was unlocked. So I turned the knob all the way and let myself in.

It may have been too early for lunch, but it wasn't too early, apparently, for happy hour. Esposito was in mid-drink from a flask.

"Can I help you?" he sputtered, wiping the corner of his mouth. He was about fifty-five, with a serious comb-over and a dirty leisure suit.

"I'm Jackie Rooney. I'm the best friend of Crystal Lake…." I couldn't quite bring myself to say of the "deceased" or "late" Crystal Lake.

"You a cop?"

"No. I'm a boxing trainer."

He took a drink from the flask again. "A girl?"

"Yeah. Long story. I got the business from my father."

"Wait, are you Sean Rooney's daughter? The champ?"

I nodded.

"Have a seat, Ms. Rooney. I was a big fan of your father's. I bet a grand on him to win his last fight against Tate. I lived the high life for a while after that fight."

I looked around his office. He must have furnished the entire thing from the Salvation Army thrift store. I wondered what he considered the high life.

"So…" he said, leaning back in his chair. The whole place had an odor of stale cigars. "How can I help you?"

"Well, I'm not sure, exactly. I understand you were Crystal's lawyer."

"That I am…er…was."

"Look, Mr. Esposito, Crystal was very dear to me. I loved her like a sister. And something doesn't add up in her death, and I'm not going to rest until I find out exactly what happened to her. So you can tell me—or not—why she came to you. But I promise you I'm not going away anytime soon. I *will* get justice for her."

"So you think she was murdered."

I nodded.

"The cops who came here, they think she was a junkie. That's the angle they're working. I think they're gonna rubber-stamp it, just dot the i's and cross the t's and say she was a drug addict."

I stared at him, willing him to open up to me.

"But you don't think she was, do you, Ms. Rooney?"

I shook my head slowly. "No sir, I don't."

He took another swig from his flask. "Neither do I."

His hands shook, and I wondered whether that was from alcoholism or the realization that he was involved with something much bigger than he could handle.

"Mr. Esposito…"

"Call me Charlie."

"Okay, and call me Jack." I took a deep breath. "Charlie, Crystal left behind a little girl. A wonderful little girl. And whatever Crystal was mixed up in, whatever was going on, she didn't deserve to be murdered. And I need to know why she came to see you."

He put down the flask, put his elbows on his desk then put his head in his hands. "She knew."

"Knew what?"

"She knew she was in danger. She literally went to the Yellow Pages, to the sleaziest part of town, to find her lawyer."

"Why?"

"Because she figured anyone legitimate wouldn't believe her—or would tell Tony Perrone she was there. Something. She knew someone like me could be bought."

"With what?"

"Money. Lots of it. She paid me $150,000 in cash to handle her final affairs."

My heart pounded in my chest. "Her…final affairs?"

"Uh-huh. She figured she might turn up dead. And she wanted someone to do her will. And if she turned up dead, she wanted to make sure you knew that it was murder and that you took care of Destiny."

"So you knew who I was when I came in here."

He nodded. "Not specifically, but I guessed as much. Most of the women who come to me are decidedly less attractive. She was here three weeks ago, you show up today, cops been sniffing around. I figured it was all connected."

"Did she say why she might end up dead?"

"She had seen something, at Perrone's house. Something bad going down. And she knew her life wasn't worth two cents."

"What?"

"I don't know. She was something, Ms. Rooney. She was gorgeous, but she had heart. She wouldn't tell me what she'd seen or heard, figuring then my life would be in too much danger."

"So what's in her will?"

"I can show it to you. Hey, Jackie, you're looking awful pale."

"It's nothing." I felt like I was going to throw up. I had taken two painkillers for my shoulder. "I had an injury out at my ranch yesterday and took some pain medicine on an empty stomach. Is there a ladies' room around here?"

He looked at me. "In case you hadn't noticed, this ain't a classy establishment. But there's a unisex bathroom down the hall. You need a key." He fumbled around in his top desk drawer and handed me a key with a large paper clip attached to it.

"Last door on the right."

I went out in the hall feeling queasier and queasier. The painkillers, coupled with the idea that poor Crystal knew her life was in jeopardy, upset me. And the idea that I was going to go kiss the porcelain goddess in a bathroom in Esposito's building was enough to push me over the edge. If his office was an assortment of stained furniture castoffs, I could hardly imagine what the bathroom would look like.

I unlocked the bathroom door and stepped inside, locking it behind me. The bathroom light, when I turned it on, sent cockroaches scattering. But desperate people can't be choosey. I leaned over the filthy bowl and threw up. Then I had ten minutes of dry heaves. Feeling like crap, I flushed the toilet, then I ran the water in the sink, splashing cold water on my face.

I unlocked the bathroom door and headed back to Esposito's office.

"Charlie?" I said as I walked in. "I want to thank you for talking to me—"

I stopped dead in my tracks. Charlie wasn't going to be talking to me at all. His brains were blown out all over his desk.

Chapter 8

A fast survey around Charlie's office told me someone had gone through his file cabinets, his desk, upending furniture and working in a hurry. My heart beating faster, I ran out in the hallway looking for his killer. I hadn't even heard a sound. Certainly not a gunshot or furniture being thrown. Running to the end of the hall, I spied two burly men rushing down the staircase.

"Freeze!" I yelled.

They didn't so much pause as draw their guns in one swift motion and fire at me. The shots bounced off the wall in back of me, and I ran faster, pulling my gun and trying to aim with my good arm. "Stop, you sons of bitches!" I wasn't gaining on them, and I fired off two rounds, both missing badly. They fired back and missed—but they were landing their shots a lot closer to me than I was to them.

They pushed open the front door of the building; the metal door made a loud slamming sound. I reached the door maybe thirty seconds later, in time to see them getting into a dark black Mercedes with black tinted windows. The driver got in first as I ran down the sidewalk, each step jarring my shoulder and arm and hurting like hell. The second guy took one last shot at me before ducking into the passenger side. I stopped and raised my gun carefully, aiming for the back windshield.

I hit it and the glass shattered.

But that didn't stop them. They sped off, leaving me on the sidewalk, memorizing their license plate and throwing up in the gutter.

Rob was not going to be happy with me.

"Hello?" he said, answering his cell phone.

"Hi, Rob. Do you have a minute?"

"Yeah. What's up?"

"I'm in trouble."

"What kind of trouble?" he asked warily.

I proceeded to tell him about my visit to Esposito's office.

"Hold on," he said, and put down the phone. I heard a string of expletives that, were I not a woman who spent all her time around boxers, would have made me blush and curled my hair. When he was finished screaming out curse words, he got back on the phone, slightly calmer.

"All right. I should know you by now. Where are you?"

"Heading back to the ranch."

"I'll meet you there in a few hours. In the meantime, stay out of trouble, Jack."

I arrived at the ranch and pulled up the long drive. Surveying the cars, I saw that Big Jimmy and Destiny were back, and Deacon was home. Everyone was there. I climbed out of my car and walked into the house.

"Auntie Jack!" Destiny came over to me and hugged my waist.

"Hey, kiddo," I whispered, running my hands through her hair and pulling her to me.

"Jack, you look like you've seen a ghost," Deacon said, sitting in his recliner in the den.

Big Jimmy, not a man long on words, merely nodded. I never knew whether it was his heritage—his great-great-grandfather had been a medicine man— or what it was, but he seemed able to read my mind.

"Destiny, Sovo is on kitchen duty tonight, and he's making brownies for dessert. Why don't you go help him," he said.

"Okay," she said brightly. Once again, I marveled at how she was dealing with things. Deacon said it was because she was too young to realize the permanence of her loss. The real challenge would be a week from now, a month from now, two years from now. I knew we'd stop at nothing to get her the best help money could buy.

"What's up, Jack?" Deacon asked. He was reading the Bible.

"Can you, Big Jimmy and I go in the office?"

"Sure." They followed me and we walked down the long hallway. Safely inside, I shut the door behind us and turned to face them.

"Things are getting worse. A lot worse." I pulled the gun out of my waistband.

"What are you doing with that?" Deacon demanded.

"Protecting myself."

"From what?"

"You both better sit down."

They did as I asked, and I told them everything that happened from arriving at Esposito's office and finding him drinking before noon, to throwing up, to the gunfight.

"What was the license plate number?"

I had memorized it by matching the letters up with words. "Destiny-Charlie-Ranch-1-7-9."

Deacon wrote it down: DCR-179.

"Not that I think we'll get any sort of match," I said. "These guys are too powerful."

Big Jimmy had said nothing, but I could see him furrowing his brow and thinking.

"What, Jimmy?"

"She said she overheard Perrone and Bonita talking about fixing the fight."

"Uh-huh."

"But this is Vegas. It's a world of corruption and fixing, card-counting, people trying to one-up the house."

"So what are you saying, Jimmy?" Deacon asked.

"There's just got to be more."

"Well, whatever she told Esposito died with him." I shut my eyes. What a mess.

"Have you told Rob?" Deacon asked.

I nodded. "Needless to say he's not all that happy with me. He's coming out to the ranch tonight."

"Can't say as I'm very happy with you, either, Jack," Deacon said.

"Why?"

"Because you can't go off by yourself investigating this. At the very least, Big Jimmy should be with you. Your brains could just as easily have ended up on that desk. And if you can't think of yourself, think of Destiny, if she had to lose the only female caring for her right now. You're the closest thing she has to a mother, Jack."

"Well, if that's the case, the kid's in trouble," I snapped. "Besides, I grew up without a mother, and I turned out just fine."

Deacon rolled his eyes. "Stop being impossible. You remind me of your six-year-old self when you talk that way."

"Look, I'm wiped out. I'm going to take something for my shoulder and go lie down. If I'm lucky, maybe I'll pass out for a bit and when I wake up, somehow all of this will work out on its own."

I turned, hearing Big Jimmy mutter under his breath, "Don't count on it."

I headed to the kitchen. Rather than risk throwing up a painkiller, I decided several shots of tequila would serve the same purpose. I did them in quick succession and went to my bedroom and lay down on my bed. Exhaustion and the stress—and maybe the tequila—overtook me, and I fell fast asleep. I didn't even dream.

I woke up as Rob gently shook me. The room was dark—the sun had set. I sat up and wiped at my face with my hand. "Jesus, how long have I been sleeping?"

"Hours."

He leaned in close to me and began kissing me. I kissed him back, grateful for his being there, longing to make the last few days just disappear. Gently, he pulled off my top.

"Oh, Jack. Your shoulder's a mess."

I looked over at it. Big Jimmy had been right. It was the color of an eggplant.

"Does it hurt?"

I nodded.

"A lot?"

I nodded.

He kissed me more fiercely. "I'm afraid for you."

"Let's not talk about it yet."

Gently, Rob undid my bra hooks, and I lay back down as he undressed me.

"Baby," he whispered, "I don't know what I'd do if anything happened to you. I'd go out of my mind." He kissed his way down my belly, his tongue soft and probing. He licked his way up to my breasts, and my breath went out of me.

Slowly, tenderly, he slid inside me. Using his arms to support himself, he moved in and out without ever putting even an ounce of weight on me or my shoulder. Occasionally, he bent his head and kissed me.

"I love you, Jack."

"I love you, too."

It was the oddest sensation. Usually we made love in a fury. Though we'd been together three years, something about us was still combustible, and our lovemaking was always passionate, sort of furious. But with having to watch my shoulder, it was as if I was being made love *to* but couldn't fully participate. It was very erotic, having his cock sliding in and out of me, slowly, gently, building to a crescendo, without any weight on me.

"God, Jack, I'm so close."

"Me, too," I said breathily.

He moved just a tiny bit faster, and I turned my head to kiss his wrist. Then I bit it lightly. A few seconds later, we both came at the same time.

Breathless, he pulled out of me and rolled away, lying on his side. As best I could I rolled over on my good side and we faced each other, chest to chest.

"Don't say anything yet," I urged. I just wanted the moment to stay with us.

We lay there ten minutes or so, just stroking each other. He touched my face, and leaned in and kissed me on my cheek.

"Let's get up so we can figure out what to do," he said, breaking our reverie.

He helped me into a sitting position, and then I stood and pulled on a pair of sweatpants and a big T-shirt; negotiating the armholes was still difficult. He dressed in his khakis and pulled on a T-shirt, "Property of Las Vegas Police Department."

My room has a sitting area, so we went and sat on the love seat, facing each other.

"Jack, no one, of course, saw anything. Not in that neighborhood. And interestingly enough, there's no proof, anywhere, that Esposito ever had Crystal as a client."

"What do you mean? What about the business card?"

"Well, that doesn't mean anything. Someone could have given her the card. But his office has been gone over with a fine-toothed comb by the department, and no file for her exists, no appointment book indicating she was ever there. Nothing."

"Did you tell the police I was there? That he told me she came to him in trouble?"

Rob shook his head. "No. That would just be inviting a world of shit to come down on you. As it is, the bad guys know you were there."

"But I don't understand. He was murdered. Doesn't that show the police something?"

"Well, that's just it."

"What?"

"There was a gun in his hand. So it looks like he committed suicide."

"That's bullshit. I was in his office ten minutes before he was shot, Rob. He wasn't a man about to commit suicide. What? Everyone involved with Crystal Lake suddenly has a death wish?"

"I didn't say that it was gonna stick, Jack. A lot of cases *appear* to be one thing when the cops arrive, but when the coroner is done, it's something else entirely. So it may *look* like he committed suicide, but the blood spatter may indicate he was killed by someone standing five feet away and then the gun was put into his already-dead hand. But we won't know that for a little while yet."

I shivered. "These guys are starting to piss me off."

"I'm not entirely sure you're safe anymore."

"I have Big Jimmy. Terry's no slouch in the size department, and neither is Sovo."

"These guys play with guns."

"I know. Big Jimmy has some motorcycle-club friends coming tomorrow. They're going to sort of roam the perimeter of the ranch. We have just about three weeks to go to New Year's. Not to mention we've got Destiny here and have got to make an attempt at a decent Christmas."

Rob shook his head. "I feel like you're a sitting duck, Jack."

"I don't know what else to do. Terry's going to fight. He's going to win. And I'm going to watch Bonita squirm."

"That doesn't sound like a solid plan."

"No. I suppose it doesn't. Basically, I'm not safe until we figure out what Crystal stumbled on."

We heard a gentle knock on the door.

"Yes?"

"Auntie Jack?" Destiny.

"Come on in."

She entered the room dressed in a pair of jeans and a flowered shirt, her long black hair in two braids mingled with feathers and beads.

"Who did your hair like that?" I asked, smiling at her.

"Big Jimmy's friend, Mrs. White Feather."

Rob looked at me. "A friend of Jimmy's owns a horse farm. He's part Native American, and his wife is originally from a reservation in Arizona."

"You look awesome, Destiny. Did anyone ever tell you that with your hair that way, you look like a Native American?"

"That's what Mrs. White Feather said. She was very, very nice."

I looked over at Destiny. She did look like a Native American princess. Which got me thinking… just who was her father? She didn't have blue eyes or blond hair like her mother. Could Big Jimmy be her father? I didn't think so. The dates didn't match up.

"Well, honey, you probably should get ready for bed."

"Will you tell me a story?"

"I don't know any."

"You don't even know Little Red Riding Hood?"

I stood and helped her find a pair of pajamas. "No. I don't even know Little Red Riding Hood. When I was a little girl, my father and Uncle Deacon told me stories about boxers."

"No fairy princesses?"

"No fairy princesses."

"Where is your father?"

"He lives a little bit away from here. It's a long story."

"What's he like?"

I thought about it. "He was the most wonderful father in the world. And he's very smart and..." My voice trailed off. That was it. If anyone could shed some light on what to do and how to do it, my father could. I would drive to the penitentiary and tell him the whole story and see what he thought I should do.

Chapter 9

I listened to Uncle Deacon for a change and asked Big Jimmy to make the drive out to the prison with me. We didn't speak much, both lost in our thoughts. Rob had spent the night, so we had pulled out the bed from the love seat—and tucked Destiny in. Rob had told her a story about Rapunzel.

That morning, there was nothing in the news about Esposito's murder or suicide. Either way, in a city of high rollers, a sleazy attorney was small news. Big Jimmy and I listened to the radio to pass the time. He drove. My arm still hurt, and I couldn't raise it up at all.

After about an hour on the road, I decided to ask him. "Hey, Jimmy?"

"Yeah?"

"After you and Crystal broke up, did you ever see her again?"

He looked out the window to his left, then straight ahead at the road. He sighed. "She had a tendency to call me when she was real unhappy."

"Over what?"

"Usually a guy."

"I used to tell her you were the best thing to ever happen to her."

"Thanks."

"What would happen when she called?"

"We'd meet somewhere, have a few drinks. She'd tell me her problems."

"Ever…you know…"

"Sometimes. I loved her, Jack. And even after she got together with Perrone, I always figured one of these days she'd come to her senses and come back to me."

I looked at him and noticed him clenching and unclenching his jaw. "I'm so sorry, Jimmy. I guess in all the commotion, and taking care of Destiny and all, I forgot that you might really be grieving hard for her."

He nodded.

"Jimmy?"

"Hmm?"

"After she got together with Perrone, did you ever…?"

"The last time I slept with her was six months before she died. Perrone was cheating on her—again.

You know, I don't want it to sound like she was using me. It wasn't like that."

"I know."

"She had such a good heart, Jack, you know that. But she was a lost soul. It was easy for her to be confused about Perrone, about me. Her father had filled her head when she was a little girl with how she was never going to amount to anything, how she was an ugly duckling. And Perrone was turning her into a swan. She was *somebody* when she was headlining that show. She was a star."

"That she was."

"I loved her."

"I know you did." I reached over and patted his arm, staring at his profile. Even from the side, Destiny looked an awful lot like him.

While Big Jimmy waited in the car, I passed through a metal detector, was frisked, herded into a waiting-area holding pen, and eventually got to sit with my father face-to-face at a cafeteria-style table. There were rules against touching each other—so no holding hands—but the guards in general didn't mind. They were mostly looking for women sitting on men's laps, trying to have sex in public. Periodically, my father patted my hand as I told him everything that had transpired.

When I finished unburdening myself, he leaned back in his chair. "You've got to find out what it is she took from Benny Bonita. Did he give any hint?"

I shook my head. "And since we weren't prepared for him, I didn't flush him out."

"That's one idea."

"What?"

"Flush him out. Call him and ask for a sit-down of some sort. You'll discuss the handoff of his stuff in return for his leaving you and Destiny alone."

"But the truth is, we have no idea what he wants."

"True. But that doesn't mean you can't play along."

"Considering we're in a world of shit, that's as good as any plan I have."

"I'm sorry, Jack."

"What are you sorry for? You have nothing to do with this. It's Bonita."

"That's not entirely true."

The room was full of women and children visiting inmates. The place was a cacophony of both misery and small flashes of happiness as loved ones were together for their allotted afternoon.

"What do you mean that's not entirely true?"

"Well…" My father looked off into the distance, at nothing, and then returned his gaze to me. I hated seeing him in his orange prison jumpsuit.

"Well what, Dad?"

"I haven't been entirely truthful about your mother."

"My mother? What could she possibly have to do with this?"

"Quite a bit, actually."

"Am I going to want to hear this?"

"Not exactly. But I never dreamed it would place your life in jeopardy."

"You're scaring me, Dad."

He folded his hands and leaned in across the table. "Your mother was indeed a cocktail waitress. She was, as I've always told you, beautiful. In almost every way, you look exactly like her. She wore her hair differently, and she carried herself differently, but she was a dark-haired beauty just like you."

"I'm listening."

"Deacon and I, we were rising young hotshots. We were Vegas's golden boys, up-and-coming boxers, brothers. The ways they could spin the story were endless."

I knew about spin. Sovo got plenty of ink because of what he'd experienced in his home country. All boxers have a myth that goes along with them, mainly young punks rising up out of the ghetto. The myth may be mostly true—most boxers come from a hard-luck life—but the media, their agents and managers, spin the story so that people get caught up in the gladiator-like fable of it all.

"Anyway, Deacon and I walked into the lounge of one of the casinos, and I take one look at Connie and she takes one look at me, and we're goners."

"I've already heard this part before," I snapped, annoyed. I hated hearing about my mother.

"I suppose you have. Well, I fell madly in love

with her, and next thing you know, we were all over Vegas, hitting the tables, living the high life."

"And?"

"And she neglected to tell me she was married to a man named Benny Bonita."

My jaw dropped, and I sat there in stunned silence. I felt like I had gotten on a roller coaster and just been dropped six stories and was on my way to riding upside down. "I beg your pardon?"

My father just nodded.

"And can someone please tell me why you've neglected to mention this teensy-tiny little fact until now? Please? Hmm? Hello? I'm listening!"

"She and Benny got a quickie divorce, and I was too stupid to realize if she played him, she'd play me. By the time we made it to this little wedding chapel, she was pregnant with you."

"Dad, I can't believe you stole Benny Bonita's wife."

"Jack, I'm being totally square with you. She wasn't wearing a wedding ring when I met her. I had no idea. I never even laid eyes on Benny until the night he beat her up but good. He was furious with her, and by attrition, me. I was so blinded by love, I took one look at her black eye and went and beat the shit out of him. I never stopped to think how he felt. I just loved her like crazy."

I felt sick. "How could you not tell me this?"

"Because she left town not five weeks after you were born. She divorced me and married a film producer who was supposedly going to back her and make her into a movie star. I guess I didn't want to talk about her. I don't know."

"So whatever happened to her?" I remembered being a little girl and feeling very curious about her. All I had were a few photos. Then, when I was thirteen or fourteen, and generally being a royal bitch in the middle of puberty, I had fantasies of her realizing she loved me after all and coming to sweep me away to Hollywood.

"I kept tabs on her for a while. I suppose I was as stupid as Benny. I figured sooner or later, she'd come back to you and me. But that producer was an adult-film guy. She lasted with him long enough to make a couple of movies. Then she moved on again. Ended up with a recording executive, made her way up the food chain once more. Then, the very last I ever heard about her, in a weird twist of reality, she was living with a yogi in a commune in Northern California."

"A yogi?"

"Yeah, a British guy. First he was into Scientology. Then he became a yogi. Part huckster, part spiritual guru. He started some kind of community. Flaky. She supposedly found God. Who the hell knows? If she found God, for real, she would have come back and made things right with you. She never had any other children."

"So this whole thing with Benny Bonita is a thirty-two-year-old grudge over a woman?"

"Partially. Yes."

"You beat him up over my mother."

"That would be correct."

"And why didn't this old grudge come out at your trial?"

"Because I just didn't see the sense in enlightening my lawyers about it. It's water under the bridge. It had nothing to do with the issue at hand."

"Nothing?"

"Well, something and nothing."

"So you and Bonita said nothing."

"Correct."

"And Deacon kept his mouth shut, too."

"We didn't want to upset you."

I shook my head. "And you didn't think one day, someday, I would find out about this?"

"Perhaps that was an error on my part. It's just that—"

"What!" I snapped.

"All these years later, I still remember looking down in your crib—me and Deacon—and we didn't even, between us, know how to change a diaper. We didn't know how to feed you. We knew nothing. And that terror…it was more frightening than anything I ever faced in the ring. Period. And I guess I've spent my whole life trying to protect you from knowing too much about your mother, about what kind of person she was. And maybe we should have told you some of this sooner."

"Maybe?" I felt like I had just discovered I was adopted. These family secrets were the types of things I should have known.

"Well, definitely. What do you want me to say, Jack? I screwed up. I'm locked up in here, and I can't even hug my own daughter."

I looked across the table at him. His time in prison had made him pale, and he definitely had more gray hair than when he went in. "How bad was Benny Bonita in love with my mother, Dad?"

"About as bad as I was."

"So in other words, he's not going to rest until he's destroyed everything in your life. Including me."

My father's eyes filled with tears. He nodded. "I'm so sorry."

I softened. "Like you said, Dad, it was a long, long time ago." I reached across the table and squeezed his hand. "I love you."

"Thank you," he whispered.

We sat like that, neither one of us talking, for a long time. I think neither one of us trusted our voices. Mine was tight, and I knew if I started crying, he'd lose it. Eventually, a harsh buzzer announced the end of visiting hours. We both stood, and I walked around the table and hugged him. Fuck the rules.

"You are the best father a girl could ask for. We'll get through this."

He nodded, wouldn't look at me. Then he filed off with the rest of the prisoners.

Out at the car, Big Jimmy was leaning on the hood. "Don't turn around but we got company."

"Oh?" I arched an eyebrow.

"Two o'clock. Mercedes sedan. Black, black-tinted windows."

"Bonita's boys?"

"I'm not too sure about that. I think they're Perrone's guys."

"Why?"

"Bonita arrived with his guys in Hummers. As far as I know, that's all Bonita and his crew ever drive. Now, Perrone, he seems like he would be the type of guy to have a bullet-proof Mercedes sedan."

"Shit."

"My sentiments exactly."

"We can't outrun them on the open road."

"Precisely. So I have an idea."

"What?"

"How good a shot are you?"

"Judging by yesterday at Esposito's office, terrible."

"Hug me."

"What?"

"Pretend like we're not onto them. Give me a hug, make it look like we're talking and I'm comforting you."

I stood on tiptoe and hugged him as best I could with my one shoulder still giving me pain. He patted my back, then said, "I have a gun in the glove box. When we get into the car, I want you to get it out. We drive, windows down, slowly. When we get to the Mercedes, take your time, shoot out the back tires."

"I don't know if I can."

"You can. Look, it's like target practice. Just don't rush, and fire off two shots. I'm going to let go of you now. I'll drive to that end of the parking lot."

"Okay." I inhaled. He walked me over to the passenger side and opened the door, looking, to all the world, as if we were very close, maybe even lovers. Made sense. A woman's lover drives her to prison to see her father.

I opened the glove box and took out the gun, feeling how heavy it was in my hand. When Big Jimmy got in, he said, "That has a very smooth trigger. Just feel it as you fire off a shot. The clip is loaded. You ready?"

"Maybe I should drive and you fire the gun."

"Not a chance, Jack. If you miss and they chase us, we need someone at the wheel who can go to its full turning radius. With your bum shoulder, that's out of the question."

"Okay."

We rolled down the windows and slowly made our way to the exit. When we got close to the Mercedes, I put the gun out the window slightly and aimed for one of the back rear tires, closing one eye as I looked down the barrel. Steadily I squeezed the trigger.

"Bingo!" I said as one tire blew.

"Other tire, Jack," Big Jimmy urged.

I fired again and missed. Then we saw the windows opening.

"They're going to fire at us!"

"Stay calm and try one more shot." He was driving so slow it seemed as if we were in neutral. Slowly I aimed—and shot out the other rear tire.

"Slam it, Jimmy!"

His foot went to the floor, and he gunned the engine. Our tires squealed and we tore out of the parking lot, our car tipping to the side as we swerved onto the road.

"Woo!" I screamed. "Amen to that! Get us home, Jimmy."

He focused on the road, a grin on his face. But for both of us, outsmarting Perrone's guys was only slightly satisfying. With guys like Perrone and Bonita after us, they would never give up. Ever. Until they had what they wanted.

If only we knew what that was.

Chapter 10

When we got home, I demanded a meeting with my uncle behind closed doors.

"Your father told you, didn't he?" he said when we were alone in the office.

"Deacon, how could you leave me in the dark like this?"

"It was what your father wanted. I think he was ashamed that he was so fooled by her."

"That's fine, Deacon. That's fine when my best girlfriend doesn't turn up dead, when I don't go see her lawyer and find brains on his desk. When that sort of shit starts happening, it's time to come clean. I'm not a little girl. I'm your partner in this business, in our fighters. We have three weeks to go and too much at stake for me not to know the whole story."

"You're right."

I sat in a leather club chair. "I think Big Jimmy, Destiny and I have to leave."

"What do you mean?"

"Look, Deacon, they know we're here. And until we figure out what Crystal took, we're here like targets waiting for them to come find us. Without whatever it is they're looking for, we're just waiting to be killed. If we get out of here, that gives us some time to figure it out. And it keeps everyone else safe."

"Maybe you should take Sovo instead."

"Sovo? Why would I take Sovo?"

"He and I have had some long conversations. He used to be a sniper. In his home country."

"A friggin' sniper?"

He nodded. "Big Jimmy and his motorcycle-club friends can guard the camp, but if you're going to be off alone with that child, a sniper would be better protection."

"So you're not going to talk me out of leaving."

He shook his head. "No, I'm not."

"Why would Sovo go with me?"

"Because he will. You're my niece, and he's like a son to me. And because he lost a sister about Destiny's age in the war."

"We better run this by Big Jimmy."

"You know Destiny is his, don't you?"

The hair on the back of my neck tingled. "How do you know?"

"Just look at her."

"That's what I think. But Jimmy hasn't said anything. Do you think he knows?"

Deacon shook his head. "Not for sure. I don't think he's allowed himself to think anything so wonderful as he is father to that child. But instinctively, you see how he is with her."

"Let's talk to him and Sovo."

"Sovo first."

Sovo stood six foot three and weighed 230 pounds. He looked like a comic book rendition of a superhero, with perfectly defined muscles and a torso that narrowed at the waist, leading up to a chest of Superman proportions. He had hair the color of coffee beans and brown eyes that were so dark they looked black.

We presented everything to him.

"What about the police?"

"They're on the take. I mean, I can't prove that, Sovo, but the investigation is getting rubber-stamped."

"What does that mean?" he asked. I sometimes forgot English was his second language.

"I'm sorry. That means that the police are saying that Crystal was a drug addict, that Esposito committed suicide, and they don't want to examine any other theories."

He nodded. "And Destiny? She is in danger?"

I nodded. "Sovo, you owe us nothing. We consider you part of the Rooney family, but you don't owe us this. You've been a good fighter, a great fighter. You could be the next heavyweight champion. You'll get a title shot in the next year sometime, I'm sure of it. And if you get hurt while guarding Destiny and me, you could lose out on that title shot. Not only that, this is all about stuff that has nothing to do with you."

He held up his hands. "Deacon has taught me to leave some of my hatred in the past. He has taught me many things. But I do not forget the man I was in Kosovo. I lost my sister there, buried her in a pauper's grave. If they have marked Destiny for being hurt, then I am still a soldier. I will not let anything happen to her. Now we speak no more. I go to pack my things. What about a weapon?"

Deacon said, "You tell me what you want, and I'll see that Big Jimmy gets it in your hands by tonight."

Sovo went over to the desk and took a piece of paper. He wrote down a list of what he wanted in terms of guns and ammunition. He nodded at Deacon and left the room.

Deacon went and found Big Jimmy, and the two of them returned.

"Jimmy," my uncle began. "You know you are as dear to us as family."

Big Jimmy nodded.

"And your protection of Jack today at the prison…the two of you could have ended up dead."

"I would have fought to my dying breath."

"We know that."

Deacon was driving me nuts. I just wanted to get it out. "Jimmy, I'm taking Destiny and hiding her. I'm going on the road."

"I'm coming."

"No, you're not."

I saw a kind of cold fury pass over his face. "I am. You can't take her, Jack. She…she…"

"Say it, Jimmy. We all think it."

"She's mine."

"Did Crystal ever tell you that?"

"No. I asked her. When she got pregnant, I asked her. But she said the baby wasn't mine. She'd had a one-night stand. She was wild in those days. I believed her. Then, after she had Destiny, she ended up with Perrone. It was like her ship came in. She wouldn't let me see the baby. I think because she knew Destiny looked Native American. A shock of black hair. Darker skin. And I started thinking, what the hell am I? A cornerman in a brutal business. I've got nothing to bring to the table. And Perrone? He was buying Destiny's baby toys and strollers, had her a French nanny. Moved them out to that castle of his."

"And you never confronted Crystal again?"

He shook his head. "After a while, I told myself that the baby didn't look so much like me after all. So I stayed away. But I can feel it. She's mine, Jack. And I'm going to get DNA testing to prove it and win custody. And I'm going to take my cut from the fight, when Terry wins, and I've got enough saved to get me and Destiny a little house."

I looked at Deacon and then at Big Jimmy. "She has to be yours, Jimmy. And if she is, you'd want her safe, right?"

"She can't be safer than with her own father."

Deacon put a hand on Big Jimmy's arm. "Listen to me. Jack is my daughter—she's like my daughter. Me and her daddy, we raised her from diapers. And in this mess we've got, I want her kept safe. Sovo used to be a sniper in Kosovo. That boy, if he was faced with gunfire, has ice water in his veins. He would die before he let anything happen to Jack or Destiny. You're good, Jimmy, but Sovo is a trained assassin, a trained killer. And he'll keep them safe while you and I figure out a way to take down Bonita. I won't trust Jack with anyone else. Now, you think on that."

Big Jimmy breathed in and out a few times. I could see him wrestling with the dilemma. Finally, he gave a single nod.

"Good," Deacon said. "Now we need you to get these—" he handed Jimmy the piece of paper Sovo wrote on "—fast. Tonight. You got a man who can do that?"

Big Jimmy looked at the list. "I think so. Let me make a call. In the meantime, I'll get my guys to move out here."

He left the room.

"You better start packing, Jack. For Destiny, too. You better explain to her that you're leaving camp."

I nodded. "First, though, I'm going to have to ask her if she can think of what Bonita wanted from her mother."

"Be careful. That child's had enough trauma."

"I know. But my guess is she holds the key to this whole thing."

I watched as Destiny brushed her teeth. "You missed the back ones," I said.

"Did not."

"Yup. You did. And if your teeth rot out of your head, I'll have to drag you to the dentist. So brush the back ones."

She obliged. When she was done, she said, "You're not a mommy, are you?"

"No. Why?"

"You can kinda tell. Like having no stories. That's weird. And you...you hang around with men all the time in a smelly gym."

"Yes. It certainly is smelly."

She laughed as I found her pajamas and helped her get undressed.

"Am I a bad auntie?"

"No. Just different." Her bottom lip trembled.

"You miss your mom?"

She nodded, and silent tears rolled down her face.

"You can cry anytime you want, Destiny. You don't have to be brave." I remembered how I had forced myself to be brave when my father stepped into the ring.

"I know," she said, and her little shoulders shuddered.

"You know, they say that as long as you remember people in your heart, they're never really gone." I picked her up in the crook of my good arm and set her onto the bed. "Let's tell each other our favorite memory about your mother."

"Okay." She brightened a little.

"I'll go first. My favorite memory…hmm…I think it was after she had you. She came over with you, and she had you all wrapped up in blankets. And she sat on the couch in the den."

Destiny smiled, her eyes still moist. A stray tear rolled down her cheek. I pulled the covers up to her chin. "And…your mother was beautiful. I'd never seen anyone so beautiful in all my life. It was how her face shined. How she just would put a finger to your hand and let you wrap your fist around it."

"My turn."

"Okay, kiddo, go ahead."

"My mommy was a terrible cook."

"We had that in common."

"But she could make one thing good."

"What was that?"

"Pancakes. And she would take raisins and make happy faces by pushing them into the pancakes."

"That's really special, Destiny. So don't you forget that memory, okay?"

She nodded.

"Can I ask you something, honey?"

"Uh-huh."

"Well, you know that bad man? The one you said your mommy didn't like very much?"

"Yes."

"Can you think of something your mother may have borrowed that was his?"

Destiny bit her lip and scrunched up her face, trying to think. Finally, she shook her head.

"Okay, sweetie. I just thought I would ask."

I decided I would tell her about leaving camp tomorrow. She was fragile tonight, and I didn't want her having nightmares.

"We have to do prayers."

"Oh, yeah, I forgot."

So we went through her little prayer. "God bless Deacon, God bless Auntie Jack. Please God special-bless Big Jimmy. And please say hello to my mommy."

"My turn."

"*You* have a prayer?"

"Yeah, yeah. Don't get all excited." I shut my eyes. "God bless Sovo and keep us all safe. Amen."

"Amen."

Chapter 11

Rob wasn't too pleased that I was leaving with Sovo.

"You're going on the road, staying in hotel rooms with Superman?"

"What?"

"Oh, come on. You were the one who said that's what he looks like."

"Well...I barely notice anymore."

"Bullshit."

"Rob, jealousy really doesn't become you."

"Why? Because it's inconvenient?" He stood with his arms folded across his chest, in the yard of the ranch where we could raise our voices in peace.

"No. Because it's ridiculous. I'm going on the run for my life. For my fucking life, Rob. And I really don't need you throwing a fit because my best chance at staying alive is a hunk."

"Let me come, too."

"Are you insane? Have you finally lost it?"

"Give me a break, Jack. With you for a fiancée it's a wonder I didn't lose it a long time ago."

Now I was pissed. I grabbed him by the collar of his shirt, noticing my bad shoulder was finally hurting less. "Look, Rob, you're on the inside of the police. You're our only chance at inside dirt. You can't go on the road with me, and until we're sure the police aren't corrupt—which right now isn't looking too damn likely—I'm not sitting here waiting to be killed. And I sure as hell am not leaving Destiny here. So stick your *dick* in your pants and get over it."

"You are the most infuriating woman I have ever met."

"Well, you're not winning any popularity contests with me right now, either."

He grabbed my left hand and held it up. "Where's your ring? You took off my diamond ring? Huh? You don't want to wear it while you're off with superstud?"

"Now you've really lost it. I took it off because I was afraid with my shoulder my arm or hand might swell in the night, and then it would get *stuck*. God, you're an idiot."

We squared off against each other.

Finally, I saw his body relax. "I'm sorry Jack. I'm just freaked out by this whole thing."

"So am I."

"I've got a friend...remember Steve Greene? From college?"

"The redhead?"

"Yeah. He's in the FBI. Assigned to this area. I'm seriously thinking of asking him for a meeting. Tell him the whole lowdown and how I think the precinct's handling of this isn't kosher. Maybe he can help us."

"Do you trust him?"

"With my life."

"Use your judgment."

"Tell me you love me."

"I love you."

"And you won't fall in love with Sovo."

"Rob—"

"I know. I'm being an idiot. It's just that...since all this started, I'm reminded every *hour* how much I couldn't handle losing you."

I stepped even closer to him and snuggled in under his chin and in the crook of his arm. "Trust me. You won't lose me."

We walked inside, and I found Destiny. "Come on, sweetie. Come into our room."

"Okay."

Destiny, Rob and I made our way down the hall to the bedroom. Rob and I sat on the love seat, and I took Destiny on my lap.

"Sweetie, me and you and Sovo are going to take a little trip."

"Leave the ranch?"

I nodded.

"What about Big Jimmy?"

"He's going to stay here."

"With all those new guys?" she asked, referring to the dozen or so Harley riders who had arrived that morning.

"Yes, with all those new guys. You know that bad man?"

She nodded.

"Well, we have to get him in jail. And until he goes to jail, it's not safe for us here. But if we go with Sovo, we will be very safe, because he's a soldier."

"A good soldier?"

Rob nodded. I was relieved he was over his little jealous bit. "He's a good soldier. A very good soldier."

"So we're going on a trip?"

"Yeah. It'll be great. We'll stay in hotels. We'll go swimming in hotel pools." The ranch lacked a pool.

"Goody!"

"Exactly, kiddo. Now, let's pack up your stuff."

I took the backpack she came with, which was empty—we'd put all her clothes and toys in drawers so she'd feel more at home. I wanted to pack light.

"We'll take four outfits. You'll wear your sneakers."

"Can I take Mr. Sniffles?"

"Who is Mr. Sniffles?"

"My puppy."

"Sure."

She handed me the stuffed dog.

"And you better take some of those wiggle-worm tapes." I envisioned long days holed up in a hotel room out of sight. Though *The Wiggles* would likely drive me nuts, they would drive me fractionally less nuts than a bored child.

She handed me her five favorite tapes. I grabbed her three coloring books and a box of crayons.

"Okay, then," I said with more bravery than I felt, "off we go on our adventure."

Destiny, Rob and I walked to the foyer. Rob carried both our bags. Sovo was waiting there with Deacon and Big Jimmy. Eddie the Geek was too broken up about us leaving, so he'd gone out to the barn. He couldn't say goodbye in person. Miguel and Terry were already training out there.

Big Jimmy squatted down to look Destiny in the eyes. "I love you, Destiny. You take care."

"I know why you love me so much."

We all gaped.

"Because I love you, too," she whispered, and grabbed his neck.

Big Jimmy wiped his eyes, then stood and took off his bear-claw necklace. I'd never seen him without it. On a thick silver chain, a single polished bear claw hung. He put the necklace around her neck.

"This will keep you safe and bring you back to me."

Destiny was awed. She looked down at the necklace and then kissed it to her lips.

Rob hugged her, then me. "Call me every night."

"Okay."

Deacon handed me a small duffel bag filled with cash. We wouldn't be traceable if we didn't use credit cards.

Sovo had a large stainless steel briefcase next to him, and another even larger case next to that. I assumed they contained the items he'd listed. He was dressed in black pants and a tight black T-shirt, and he was a different Sovo from the smiling man who'd made brownies a day or so ago. I knew him as a careful boxer. Now that I was aware he was a sniper it made sense. Snipers are careful, meticulous, detail-oriented soldiers. And Sovo was a boxer who never made a move based on chance. It was as if, in the ring, he was playing chess. He never wasted a punch. But standing there, I could tell his nerves were taut.

Sovo and Rob shook hands, and then Sovo, Destiny and I went outside with everyone. We got ready to settle into a black, windowless van borrowed from one of Big Jimmy's friends. Rob kissed me goodbye.

"Be careful," he whispered.

"Solve the case," I said as I hugged him.

We settled Destiny in the back, which had a table, and she started coloring. We also had a VCR/DVD player. Sovo and I took the two captain's seats up front. He drove. I was navigator. We pulled away from the ranch, and I waved forlornly to my friends, my family. I hoped I would live to see them all again.

We had no destination in mind, though we thought vaguely that a city in California, like L.A., might be a good bet. It's easy to get lost in a city. On the other hand, according to Sovo, an isolated spot allows you to be aware of anyone coming and going.

So we flipped a coin and headed west.

Sovo drove intently. I had never spent much time alone with him. The camaraderie I had with him was usually in the gym, surrounded by the other guys. After we had been on the road about two hours, I noticed Destiny had fallen asleep. We could speak more freely.

"I can't thank you enough for this, Sovo."

He shrugged. "Men who prey on women are below my contempt."

"I know you've been through a lot. Lost a lot. I'm sorry that in some small way that violent past has to be part of the present."

"Old soldiers…you know…how do I say it? We never stop being soldiers. I can dress like this—" he took one hand from the wheel and gestured at his clothes "—but inside, I'm still a soldier. I still jump when I hear a loud noise. I still watch the doors. I still watch the horizon for the dust kicked up by a car coming down the road. It's how I was trained. It never leaves me."

I wondered if that was why, beautiful as he was,

he never had a girlfriend. I decided I hadn't earned the right to ask that question yet.

"Want me to drive?"

"No, I'm okay." He watched the rearview mirror. "Anyone follow us?"

"No. But we can't be too careful."

"No. I suppose we can't."

We drove for another four hours, until we came to a midsize town off of the highway. We pulled into a parking lot for a Holiday Inn.

"I'll go in," Sovo said. "If anyone is looking for us, you are the most obvious. You and her. No one knows me. My license doesn't even have my real name."

"Why not?"

He smiled. "In case. You know?"

I nodded. "I wish I didn't, but yeah, I know."

Our cover, we decided, was taking a trip to see the country. Husband and wife. I'd put on my engagement ring again. We would call each other "honey" and "dear" in public.

He went to the front desk. I could see him inside. He paid cash, smiled, looking for all the world like a typical dad. Albeit a drop-dead gorgeous one. He came back out and flashed me a thumbs-up. Mr. and Mrs. Holtz were checked in.

We chose the hotel for the fact that we would never have to go through the lobby. It was set up like an old-fashioned motor lodge. We drove around to the back and parked the van, and we hurriedly collected our belongings and opened the door to our room. Destiny had woken from her nap and held my hand as we surveyed our temporary home. Standard-issue hotel. Two queen-size beds, a dresser, a desk, a bathroom. Coffeemaker. Two lamps. TV.

Sovo brought in our bags and shut the door, dead-bolting it and putting on the chain. Then he seemed to remember something, opened the door again and put on a Do Not Disturb sign, relocked it all and turned around. Smiling at Destiny, he said, "Come on. We play cards."

Destiny and Sovo settled into Go Fish, and I turned on the television. ESPN was airing a little segment on the upcoming fight. Deacon was interviewed—an old tape from before the last big fight.

"It's Uncle Deacon!" Destiny squealed.

We watched the segment. Deacon sat against a backdrop of a poster from his fighting days. They flashed a picture of my father. Told the story of when they were champs, and now how they had trained a top fighter. Then Destiny said she was hungry.

I looked at Sovo. Suddenly, I realized I needed to be in sync with him at all times. Part of how we would survive was reading each other's signals. He said, "Room service. We have a picnic, okay?"

Destiny liked that idea, so we ordered her chicken nuggets and fries, and he and I each ordered a club sandwich. I longed for a shot of tequila. Something, anything, to take the edge off of being in a small room *waiting,* in some way, to be found. I kept eying Sovo's suitcases. Aside from the guns, he had a small duffel bag. He had traveled very light, except for the weapons. In their case, he traveled with a lot of fire-power.

The curtains were drawn, and the air conditioner droned. The bedspreads and curtains were a garish chintz with shades of turquoise. The rug was a dark green.

Room service knocked on the door forty minutes later. Sovo stood and crossed to the door. Putting his face to it, he said, "Just leave it by the door. I'm just out of the shower."

A muffled "Yes sir" came back. After a sev-eral-minute wait, he opened the door and took in the tray.

"Yum! I'm starving," Destiny said.

The three of us sat cross-legged on one of the beds, imitating a picnic. "Pretend you are at your fa-vorite picnic spot," I urged Destiny.

"Mommy and I used to go eat out in Uncle Tony's zoo. On a bench. It was really nice. We could hear the birds singing and even the lion roaring."

Sovo looked shyly at me. "What is your favorite spot?"

"Hmm…I guess I've never been on a picnic be-fore."

"What?" Destiny look dumbfounded. "How could you have never been on a picnic?"

"Well, I guess the closest I ever came was when we would order sandwiches for the gym and would sit around the office eating. I didn't get a whole lot of fresh air as a kid. How about you, Sovo?"

"Ah...me. Well, there was a place, near my hometown, where you could go up in the mountains and look down on the village. I would go there with my little sister and my mother sometimes, with a loaf of bread, some wine, some cheese. That was before the war. After that it wasn't safe to go outside."

"There was a war where you're from, Sovo?" Destiny asked.

He nodded.

Destiny reached out a tiny hand and rubbed his hand, hers looking miniscule next to his. "I'm sorry."

He swallowed hard and simply nodded.

After we ate, Sovo told Destiny some Kosovo fables. Then I helped her into her pajamas and settled her into the bed farthest from the door. It wasn't long before she was breathing heavily. I went into the bathroom and took a hot shower, then dressed in sweatpants and a sweatshirt. When I came back, Sovo was sitting in a straight-backed chair.

"Aren't you going to sleep?"

"In a little while."

"You need to sleep, Sovo. We need you alert, not tired."

"I know. It's just that now that I am a soldier again, it's hard to turn that off. Hard to unwind."

I walked over to where he sat. "Go lie down." I put my hands on his shoulders and kneaded them. "You're all knots."

He nodded but didn't say anything. I rubbed his shoulders for a few minutes then moved over to the bedside and climbed in with Destiny.

"Promise you won't stay awake all night?"

He nodded.

I turned out the light so that now the only illumination in the room was the glow of light from the bathroom. I wanted to leave a light on for Destiny, but I had shut the door so only a sliver glowed.

I lay next to Destiny on my side, acutely aware I was sharing the room with Sovo. I wasn't used to sleeping with another man in the room—only Rob. I shut my eyes and pretended to sleep, a tension filling me. Then I opened my eyes just a slit. Sovo was still sitting there, watching over Destiny and me.

Chapter 12

Sovo felt we shouldn't stay at the same hotel two nights in a row. "It's too easy for the maid, someone, to see you—or not see you and then be suspicious that there's no one coming and going from the room."

I agreed with him. We took backroads, driving through the West. We crossed the border into California and found another place to spend the night. He relented and let Destiny swim in the pool, but he spent the entire time motionless in an upright pool chair, his eyes surveying the doors of the hotel that opened to the pool, the rooftops and the bushes that surrounded the pool. He never relaxed, I noticed, and I felt very sorry for him, in some way, forced by a war into becoming the man he was now as opposed to the young man looking down on his village, with a loaf of bread and some cheese in a picnic basket.

This second night on the road, we elected to stop in a "suites" hotel, which gave us two rooms. We settled Destiny in for the night in the bedroom and then sat together in the kitchen-living area while Sovo gave me instructions on how to use the weapons he had brought. One gun screwed together and had four pieces. Over and over again he watched me assemble and disassemble it, timing me and making me do it faster and faster.

After so many years training fighters, where the name of the game wasn't only strength, but reflexes, I was fast. For the first time since we left, I saw Sovo break out into a big grin. "You would have been an impressive soldier," he said.

"Thanks."

Next, we stood and practiced stances. I learned how to find my line of sight. Sovo stood in back of me, his arms around me as I practiced, with an unloaded gun, how to squeeze the trigger smoothly, instead of in a fast jerking method, which had the potential of throwing off my aim. Over and over again, I practiced until it started to become second nature.

"How's your shoulder?" he whispered. He was so close to me his breath felt like a little breeze in my ear. I shivered.

"Sore, but better."

Instinctively, perhaps, without thinking, he leaned his head down and kissed my bum shoulder. Then he stepped away.

"You should get some sleep," he ordered somewhat coldly.

I ignored what he'd just done, aware there was some kind of attraction between us, and knowing it was the stress and tension of being in this situation. At least I hoped that was all it was.

"Okay. I'll see you in the morning."

"Good night." He wouldn't look at me. Now I remembered the fight he'd had with Terry. Suddenly I wondered whether he'd gotten so intensely angry because Terry had punched him too hard, or because Terry had hurt me.

I went into the bathroom and scrubbed my face and brushed my teeth. Once again, I climbed into bed with Destiny, spooning around her in the hopes of making her feel safe.

But I couldn't sleep. I wondered what Sovo was going through. Looking from the bedroom into the living room, I saw him, as usual, sitting in a straight-backed chair, a gun in his hand, alert and ready. And yet I saw him, in the darkness, look at me from time to time.

The next day, we got into the van and headed up the Pacific Coast highway. I had been checking in with Deacon and Rob twice a day. I called Deacon as Sovo drove.

"How's it going?"

"I think they may know something's up."

"Why?"

"Last night, and then again this morning, two Hummers drove on the main road, slowly past our drive. But they saw the Harleys and the guys on the perimeter and thought twice about coming in here."

"Do you think they know Destiny and I are gone?"

"I'm not sure. But Bonita most definitely knows we've got firepower out here at the ranch. Meaning he will back off—or come with even more firepower."

"Be careful, Deacon."

"I've been praying. I'm praying the Lord will smite them down."

"I'll settle for sticking them in prison."

"How's Sovo?"

I glanced over at him. "He's good."

"Do you feel safe?"

"Yeah. I do."

"Good. Tell him I said hello."

"Okay, Deacon. Talk to you later." I hung up. "Deacon says hi."

Sovo just nodded.

Next I called Rob. "Hey…"

"God, I was hoping you'd call me. Listen, Perrone seems like he's about to pull something."

"Why?"

"He was here meeting with the chief of police for two hours. Arrived with his attorney."

"Know what he was up to yet?"

"No. Not yet. But I'll find out. How's Sovo?"

Suddenly, that was the $64,000 question of the day. "He's good. I'm sure he's tired. He sits up at night watching over us. Keeping us safe."

Sovo smiled.

"Well, stay alert. Stay careful. I love you."

"Love you, too." Out of the corner of my eye, I watched Sovo's face turn serious again.

We eventually pulled into a small town, very quaint. We passed a bed-and-breakfast with a hand-painted wood sign and blooming rosebushes, and then we stopped to get gas.

"Can we get a hotel here?" Destiny whined.

"No," Sovo said sternly. He looked at me as he pumped gas, talking to me through the passenger window. "A place where everyone knows your business is not a good place to be."

I turned my head around to face Destiny in the back of the van. "Sovo says we have to drive a little farther."

"But I feel like I'm going to frow up."

"Throw up?" The thought of dealing with kid vomit scared me more than the idea of dealing with Bonita's crew. "You can't throw up." I looked at Sovo, eyes wide. "She feels like she's going to puke."

He finished pumping gas and climbed into the van. "Okay, we stop."

"But you said small towns are no good."

"They're not. But Baby says she's going to throw up. We stop."

The bed-and-breakfast was too small, but we had passed a small motel about eight miles before town, nestled in the foothills of some small mountains, so we retraced our route and got a room for the night. The motel kind of gave me the creeps. I half expected Norman Bates to pay a visit.

We got Destiny settled into a bed, found a channel that had cartoons on and gave her an empty ice bucket to throw up in. Turned out to be in the nick of time. No sooner did I hand it to her than she vomited. And then she started crying.

Me? I was in a panic. Sovo shifted into Florence Nightingale mode. He emptied the bucket and brought it back. He sat on one side of Destiny, with me on the other. Sovo put his hand to her forehead. "She's warm."

I touched her forehead and then her cheeks. "Baby, you have a fever."

Tears rolled freely down her face. "I…want… my…mommy."

She crawled into Sovo's lap, and he just soothed her. Then he began humming a tune I didn't recognize.

I stood and retrieved the van's keys from the dresser. "I'm going to the drugstore back in that town with the bed-and-breakfast. I'll get her warm ginger ale for her stomach and some Tylenol."

"I should go."

The idea of dealing with a puking child wasn't appealing to me. But I could've handled it, I suppose.

In truth, I decided I'd rather he be protecting Destiny at the Bates hotel than me. I couldn't shake the feeling that we were too vulnerable.

"Take the g-u-n," he spelled out. "The one with the laser light. It's going to be dark soon."

I opened one of the suitcases and withdrew a gun, black and sleek. I put a clip in just as Sovo taught me, and took the safety off. It was equipped with a red laser beam to help align shots in the dark. I left the room, and I heard Sovo double-lock the door behind me.

Driving the van back to the small town, I glimpsed the sun just beginning its descent. It was stunning; the sky was almost purple in spots. I tried to take deep breaths. I wanted to be back home, at camp, with the guys. I wanted to be training Terry and preparing for what should have been the biggest night of my life. And most of all, I wanted my life back. My real life. Not this pretend life with bad guys and good guys and snipers and guns.

In the store, I followed Sovo's instructions. Each night when Destiny slept, he offered training in what made a good sniper, and what made a good soldier. In the drugstore, I was neither so unfriendly that I attracted attention or seemed antisocial, nor was I so friendly that anyone would remember our conversation. I didn't ask any questions of anyone. I tried not to act nervous, or as Sovo put it, "shifty." I bought ginger ale and children's Tylenol. I also picked up a new coloring book and a deck of Old Maid cards. We were all getting sick of Go Fish.

When I got back into the van, I made a right, heading through town, back to the Bates motel. If nothing else, this trip would provide many a good story to tell my father and Deacon.

I pulled into the gravel parking lot. It was then that I saw it. Far away, way down the parking lot, was a Hummer.

"Shit!" I didn't know what to do. Go on inside— and lead them right to Destiny. Drive off in the van— and eventually they'd overtake me and I'd have left Sovo and Destiny stranded without a vehicle. And yeah, there was that little thing that I'd be *dead*. I turned off my lights and called Sovo's cell phone.

"Hello?" he answered.

"Me. We've got company."

"All right. I get ready for them. Where are you?"

"Right outside. I've got an idea, though. You cover Destiny."

"What are you doing?"

"Making like a sniper."

"Careful."

It was still light enough that I could see. I climbed out of the van, stood, and then acted as if I'd forgotten my room key. Then I went down the sidewalk and through the pass-through that was by the hotel front desk. I backtracked through the pool area, hiked a bit on a canyon trail, and ended up above the Hummer. I tucked into some scrub brush, well out of sight.

Sovo had taught me that a sniper is patient. I could be that.

A sniper doesn't force a shot. Allowing for movement, a sniper waits for the *perfect* shot. I would wait.

The guys in the Hummer turned out to number just two. They eventually emerged from the vehicle as the last fingers of light stretched across the sky. They both wore shoulder holsters around their white dress shirts, and then they put on their jackets. They had on dark sunglasses. And they were big—they looked easily the size of Sovo.

I used the gun to line up a shot, but the perfect shot never presented itself. They conferred outside the Hummer, with the vehicle blocking them a bit. Then they talked on their cell phones. Never hanging up, they made their move toward the hotel room. I think maybe they figured they missed me returning, or there was a back entrance to our room. They strode confidently.

I aimed the gun at the bigger guy, deciding that though I wanted my old life back, I didn't want to kill a man in cold blood to get it. I would kill them if I had to. But for now, I was content to shoot them in the leg. The red beam from the laser sight traveled through the darkening light. I heard Sovo's voice in my head: Squeeze smoothly; be one with your weapon. I had teased him that he was the Zen sniper. But I breathed and, in some way I can't fully explain, the crickets' cacophony receded. The scrub brush stopped itching at my arms. The slight chill to the air ceased to cause me to shiver. The beam hit the bigger man's thigh, and gently, (allowing, as Sovo had taught me, for movement,) I squeezed the trigger. The man crumbled and screamed out.

The other man immediately withdrew his weapon and waved it wildly about. I had a clear shot at his chest. But I wasn't a killer. I would have to leave that to real soldiers. I let the shot pass and watched as he helped the wounded man to his feet, letting him lean on his shoulder as he limped, badly, to their Hummer. They climbed inside and sped away.

I knew that chances were more than one pair of men had scouted us out. We needed to move, and we needed to move fast. They were likely on their cell phones revealing our whereabouts at the Bates Motel.

Racing down from my hiding spot, I ran to our room and pounded on the door.

"It's me, Sovo! Open up!"

He opened the door a crack and then threw it wide. He was all packed. A mattress was turned over, hiding Destiny, and he had a gun strapped to his chest and a knife to his calf.

Within minutes we were in the van. I climbed in the back and settled Destiny in with a stolen hotel blanket. She was shivering. I opened the bag containing the Tylenol, almost forgotten in the melee. Sovo drove us out on the highway, heading toward a more populous area.

"Destiny, how much do you weigh?" I asked, looking at the label.

"I don't know."

"Okay, we'll go by age." I measured off a dose in the little plastic cup it came with and handed it to her. "Drink up, Baby."

She sipped.

"Does it taste bad?" I asked.

"No. Tastes like bubblegum."

"Really?" I stuck my finger in the medicine and lo and behold, it really did taste like bubblegum. "Wow! They didn't have this when I was a kid."

Sovo sped down the road, focused and intense. I sat by Destiny, who lay across the couchlike bed in the back.

"Will you rub my tummy?" she asked, her voice tremulous.

"Sure, honey." I began moving my hand in a circular motion across her tummy, slowly, soothingly.

"What's happening?"

"The bad guys found us, but Sovo and I took care of it, so don't be afraid."

"What do they want?"

"I wish I knew, Destiny, I wish I knew."

I rubbed her belly until she fell asleep. Thank God she didn't throw up again.

I settled into the passenger seat beside Sovo. He kept looking in his rearview mirror.

"I'm not sure how they found us."

"Me, neither. Luck, maybe."

"What happened?"

"I crossed through by the front desk, climbed

back around the canyon trail and up into the scrub. I lined up the laser beam and pulled off a lucky shot."

"Guess both sides have luck today."

I nodded. "I shot him in the leg. I had a clear shot at the chest of the second guy, but I didn't take it." I looked out the passenger-side window.

"Good," said Sovo.

"Good?"

"Killing a man is for snipers and soldiers. You're a boxing trainer. When this is over, you should go back to your life without the memory of killing."

"I guess I knew if he came through the door, you'd take care of him."

Sovo nodded. We drove on into the night in silence, acutely aware that we had better figure out soon what Benny Bonita wanted. Because next time, we might not be so lucky at all.

Chapter 13

By morning, taking shifts, we had closed in on the city of Los Angeles.

"We have to be careful," I told Sovo.

"Of what?"

"Gridlock."

"What is gridlock?"

"That," I explained, as we drove over an overpass and I pointed down at mile after mile of stuck, unmoving traffic.

"Accident?" he asked.

"Nope. Just L.A."

"This is crazy! Why would people live like this? Like rats in a maze."

"You'll see."

The weather was glorious, and I had been to L.A. several times for fights, so I knew my way around. I maneuvered over to Melrose. As we drove down the street, women in miniskirts that rode high enough to see their crotch, and low enough to see the strings of their thongs, walked along perched on stiletto heels, with little dogs in purses.

"*This* is why people put up with gridlock."

Sovo's eyes grew wide. He may have been a sniper, he may have been guarding Destiny and me like a hero, but he was still a guy with a frigging pulse.

We drove along, taking in the sights. We passed the Farmer's Market, and then I drove until we could see the big Hollywood sign. Destiny was still sleeping in the back, but soon she began to rouse.

Sovo climbed in back and felt her head. He'd been checking her almost hourly. "Just a little warm," he said cheerfully. "Hello, Baby," I heard him say to her.

"Hello, Sovo."

"We're in L.A. We going to be big shots. Movie stars."

Destiny giggled.

"You want to watch those worms?"

"*The Wiggles,* Sovo. *The Wiggles.*"

"Okay. You watch them? We'll find a place to stay soon."

"I'm getting kind of bored with *The Wiggles.*"

I piped up from the driver's seat. "Destiny, honey,

that's all we brought. When we stop, I'll find a place to buy you a few new videos. You'll have to tell me which ones you like."

"Oh, no, that's okay, Auntie Jack. I have some other ones. In the *Wiggles* boxes. I want to watch the ones with my mommy on them."

"The what?" Frantically I looked for a place to park. I backtracked to a shopping mall and parked in the farthest spot in the lot. I turned off the car and climbed in back.

"Destiny," I said, shaking her by the shoulders. "What did you say, honey?"

"I want to watch the ones with my mommy in them."

"Show us," Sovo said hoarsely, nervously.

Destiny went over to her pink backpack and produced four *Wiggles* boxes. She had been watching the same one over and over and over again for days. I hadn't even thought to ask her why she didn't watch the other four. Inside the tape boxes, which carried the bright, attractive, colorful *Wiggles* group on the front, were tapes marked Security 1, Security 2, Security 3 and Security 4. Crystal wasn't such a dumb blonde after all. She had taken them for insurance of some sort.

I popped the first one in. It was surprisingly high definition for tape from a security camera, but then again, it was from Tony Perrone's inner sanctum, his office. He'd have the best security money can buy. But why would he tape his own office? I turned up the volume as Crystal walked in and gave him a kiss. Destiny beamed as she sat next to me. She pointed to the TV screen and tugged on Sovo's shirt. "That's my mommy."

"Very beautiful," he said, nodding.

On the tape, Crystal sat on Tony's lap, and they murmured and kissed. They discussed vacation plans—skiing in Switzerland. And Crystal wanted to try out her French with a stop on the Riviera and Nice. They talked about Destiny, her nanny, the expensive private kindergarten she would attend in the fall, redecorating her room…Crystal had found an incredible muralist who would turn it into a fantastical fairyland.

After about ten minutes, Crystal kissed Tony passionately and left the office, perched on her Jimmy Choos. We fast-forwarded through boring minutes of tape where Tony simply sat at his desk working on his laptop, making calls, shuffling through papers. A secretary brought him coffee. He pinched her ass. What a guy.

Next, Benny Bonita came into the office. He said he had a consortium of gamblers who were going to pool their money in several large bets on several upcoming fights—Miguel Jimenez, four fighters of which I owned no part of, and the big one…Terry Keenan. To ensure things went the way the consortium needed, Benny would, necessarily, persuade the boxers in question. He would go after their families. In Terry's case, Bonita said they had already virtu-

ally secured his cooperation through a crooked
drug deal.

"What do you mean?" Perrone asked on the tape.

"Our good old police chief, Larry Dillard had his
two cops entrap the dumb lug. But of course, our
guys were clever. The tapes are carefully rehearsed.
Keenan's brother is entrapped *before* he gets on film.
Just like with Sean Rooney."

"Son of a bitch," I muttered.

"Auntie Jack," Destiny scolded.

"Sorry, kiddo."

We watched the end of tape one. Crystal came
back on screen briefly. She told Tony she was frightened of Bonita, and he told her not to worry her
pretty little head about it.

Yeah. That was how poor Crystal lost her pretty
little life.

We opted for a room on the first floor of a French
hotel near the Beverly Center. We were tired of motor
lodges, tired of the road, but elated that we now had
something on Bonita. And the chief of police, Lawrence Dillard. And Perrone. It still didn't prove they
murdered Crystal, but tape one alone would surely
cause Perrone to lose his casino license. It would destroy his empire. And Bonita would be looking at
time. As for the chief, he wouldn't be chief for long.
I also thought I had a good shot at getting my father
cleared.

My elation faded, however, and the realization of

all this gave me a major headache. We were now up against both a crooked police chief, his staff and two powerful men. And they had everything to lose. Money, prestige…freedom.

I gave Destiny a bath. Her fever seemed to have abated, but she was still a little pale. A good night's sleep in a bed that wasn't *moving* like the van would do her a world of good. It would also do me a world of good.

I pondered her name. "Hey, kiddo, did your mom ever tell you why she named you Destiny?"

"Yes, Auntie Jack," she said as I took a washcloth and scrubbed her back with a rich oatmeal soap. Nothing like a luxury hotel.

"How come she named you that?"

"Because Mommy said she had a hard life. Her mom and dad weren't very nice to her. Her daddy drank too much. My mommy was very sad. And she said when she found out she was going to have a baby, she figured out that all she'd gone through was worth it if it meant she got to have me. That I was her destiny."

My eyes welled up, and I took my sleeve and wiped at them. I poured shampoo onto Destiny's long black hair and began scrubbing. "Your hair sure is pretty, sweetie," I said.

"Don't you think my hair looks like Big Jimmy's?"

"I do. I really do. It's long and black and shiny."

"Do you like Big Jimmy?"

"Yes."

"A lot?"

"Yes."

"As much as Sovo?"

"Yes."

"As much as Rob?"

"Well, I like them in different ways. Rob is my boyfriend, and Big Jimmy and Sovo are my friends."

"Rob told me he was your fiancé. He said you're going to marry him."

"Well, unfortunately, that's a long way off. See, I want my daddy to be there. Your mom's dad was a bad man, but my dad, he's a good guy."

She lay down in the water and floated on her back, her hair splayed out. She whispered, "I think Sovo is in love with you."

"No…that's silly. Why would you say that?"

"The way he looks at you. Only when you're not looking at him."

Great. Just what I needed. A pint-size psychologist.

She rolled over and splashed in the water. "I like this hotel a lot."

"Me, too."

"So do you think Big Jimmy would be a good dad like your dad, or a bad dad like Mommy's dad?"

"Oh, sweetheart, Big Jimmy would be the gentlest, most wonderful father in all the world. I've known him since I was nine years old. He was eighteen or nineteen, I think. And he was one tough cookie, but inside he was a good, good man just waiting to be reborn. And if I had to pick, of all the people I know and of all the people your mother knew, one man to be your father, I would pick Big Jimmy."

"If he really is my new dad, then I would get to see you all the time."

"Hmm. I hadn't thought about that. Then I am extra glad about that."

"I love you, Auntie Jack."

I looked down at her and smiled. "I love you, kiddo."

"Why do you call me kiddo?"

"'Cause I'm a boxing trainer. We're supposed to be tough and not get all mushy."

"That's silly."

"I suppose it is."

After all the "road food" we'd eaten, we attacked our room service with gusto. We ordered delicious baguettes and a bottle of red wine, filet mignon and Destiny's usual—chicken nuggets.

Destiny curled up on the goose-down pillow, and I tucked the soft, rich blanket up under her chin. Her hair was still a tiny bit damp, and it smelled of the hotel shampoo, a combination of ginger and rosemary scents.

After she was sound asleep, Sovo and I turned to the VCR that came with our television, and we sat on the other bed, up against the pillows, and watched tapes two, three and four. I sipped a little bit of red wine. Sovo even had half a glass, not wanting more, which might cloud his judgment. He still wore a holster with a gun in it.

I had to hand it to Crystal, she orchestrated the cameras, then took the tapes that would collapse Perrone's empire. The other three tapes revealed his ties to organized crime—as well as Chief of Police Lawrence Dillard's ties to the Mob. Christ, the tapes showed such an intersecting maze of corruption and greed, the fallout would reverberate for a long time to come.

Sovo watched, his face scrutinizing the men.

"What are you doing?"

"What do you mean?"

"You're staring so hard at the television."

"One, a sniper observes his enemies, Jack. Never forget that. Is Perrone right- or left-handed?"

I shrugged.

"Where does the chief wear his gun? Where does Perrone keep his gun?"

"Oh, I know that one. Bottom drawer, right-hand side."

"What about his other guns?"

"What other guns?"

Sovo rewound the tape a minute or two and in a split second Perrone opened a coat closet in his office, and barely visible, for a flash on the screen, was a long rifle or gun of some sort in the closet.

"So, one, I must watch to know my enemy."

"And two?"

"I will memorize the face of the men who tried to do harm to Destiny—and you."

We watched in silence awhile. When I saw the determination on his face, I had to ask. "How did your little sister die?" I whispered.

He stiffened, holding his shoulders ramrod straight. "She stepped on a land mine. I do not even have the face of the bastards who took her life."

I patted his leg. "I'm so sorry, Sovo."

"It seems like a lifetime ago."

"I can only imagine. My life prior to Crystal getting killed seems like light-years away…. Is that why you don't have a girlfriend?"

He shrugged. "Just don't meet the right kind of girls. From what I see, Vegas is like L.A. No?"

I grinned. "Yes. Similar."

"Besides, what woman wants to lie with a killer in her bed?"

"Sovo, any woman who didn't understand your life in Kosovo would be a fool."

"Thank you."

I looked at his profile. "No. Thank you. For everything."

"We need to make several copies of the tapes," he said grimly.

"For insurance?"

"Yes. Because I have a feeling these men will stop at nothing."

"I was afraid you'd say that."

I felt my eyelids grow heavy with wine, exhaustion and worry. I must have fallen asleep. I woke up at two in the morning. The TV was a fuzzy gray signal from the tape being over, and I felt nothing next to me. Sitting up, disoriented, I realized Destiny was in her bed, and I was in Sovo's. I looked over at the club chair in our room. Sovo was asleep, his gun on the table next to him. I got up and pulled the bedspread from the bed and gingerly placed it on him. At my touch, he woke, grabbed his gun, cocked it and aimed toward the door in what seemed like two seconds.

"Sovo! It's me."

Both of us were frightened out of our minds. My heart pounded rapidly, and I could even hear my blood throbbing in my ears.

"I'm so sorry, Jack."

I was breathless from the fright. Inhaling, I said, "I should have known better. I was just bringing you a blanket. Why don't you sleep in the bed, and I'll watch the door."

"No. We all sleep."

"Okay." I walked over to where Destiny slept and climbed in. I had a crick in my neck from sleeping propped up on the headboard.

"'Night."

"'Night." Sovo stripped down to boxers and a T-shirt and, gun under his pillow, went to sleep in his own bed. I felt sorry for him. And more than anything, I just wanted to be able to go home.

Chapter 14

The next day, I strapped a gun to my ankle, left the hotel and took the van. I went shopping and bought a VCR, multiple blank tapes, mailing envelopes and new videotapes for Destiny. I was sick of *The Wiggles,* so I opted for several Disney movies. As I walked around, I thought of how odd it felt to have a weapon on me. It took me an hour or so before I stopped looking guilty, I think. I almost felt like looking at the faces of other people to see if they guessed I was "packing heat." After a while, I got used to it. I was only half aware the gun was there. I kept thinking of Sovo's advice to be "one" with the gun.

Driving back to the hotel, I parked the van half a block away, unwilling to entrust our sole vehicle to a valet in case we had to leave in a hurry. I strolled the block and walked through the gracious lobby of our hotel, which smelled of fresh purple-colored hyacinth in vases. When I reached our room, Sovo opened the door when I knocked four times—our little code. I felt like a spy.

We set up the new VCR with extra wiring hooking it up to the hotel's VCR in order to make copies of the tapes. I had called the ranch, and Eddie the Geek, who was a gadget freak, walked me through setting it up. He'd say things like "Put the red wire in the red hole and the yellow wire in the yellow hole." I didn't even *know* VCRs had color-coordinated holes.

Sovo and I spent all day making three copies of each tape. I addressed one set to Rob, one to Deacon and one to Big Jimmy. Then I took them to a post office and paid for next-day service to all my recipients. I kept the originals and packed them in the false bottom of Sovo's larger gun case.

We decided to leave in the morning. Room service dinner was again delicious. Destiny fell asleep early. She had been a good sport all day, happy to watch the videos for the odd glimpses here and there of her mother. Destiny's fever was totally gone, and I figured with something to bargain with, we could now go back home. Sovo went to the ice machine, and I called Rob.

"We found what Bonita wants."

"What?"

"Security tapes from the Perrone mansion of him and Tony arranging gambling on fixed fights."

"Not surprising. It's the most corruption-prone sport in the world."

Of course it was. Two men, two gladiators, boxing in a canvas ring. Last man standing wins. If one of those men is corruptible, he can take a dive, thus fixing the fight—not only the winner or loser of the fight, but what *round* he goes down in—which impacts bets placed on the fight, depending on the odds the Las Vegas bookmakers set. And only one man needs to take the dive, the bribe. One man. It's thus much easier to fix a fight than to, say, fix a football game, where the one man the Mob may own is just one of a million variables down on the field.

"That's not all."

"There's more?"

"Chief Dillard is on the tapes. And the tapes exonerate my father."

"Christ, Jack. Crystal stepped into it big-time. You're going to bring down an awful lot of big shots with these tapes. Where'd you find them?"

"In the cases of Destiny's kid videos."

"Well, the feds will be interested in hearing this story."

"If I live to tell it."

"Look, I'm going to talk with my FBI buddy. I can't bring you in to the police. So we go the FBI route."

"What about a reporter?"

"Last resort. That's in the movies. This is reality. The feds will help you."

"I don't know. Except for you, considering what happened to my father, it's not easy for me to trust men with badges."

"Jack, we have to cooperate with the authorities."

"I know. Somewhere down in my gut, I know. This also explains something."

"What?"

"No Amber Alert. The burying of this whole story in the media. They don't want Destiny found. They don't want me found. They want to find me themselves and kill me for these tapes. Perrone insisted Destiny was safe and it was a 'family matter' and the chief just went along with it? They want us all to drive off a canyon road. Something. Anything. Just keep us quiet."

"Stay smart, stay careful. I'll talk to you tomorrow. Hopefully by then I'll have a plan."

"Hopefully. You'll also have something else."

"What?"

"Insurance. I'm mailing you the tapes."

"What?"

"Yeah. You, Deacon and Big Jimmy. You're each getting a set."

"Please be careful, Jack. You're playing with fire."

"Yeah, well, they started it."

The next day, reluctantly, we left the cocoon of our fancy hotel room. We packed, took the VCR I bought and headed up the block to the van after settling our bill. Climbing in, I offered to drive.

"I can drive," Sovo said, waving me off.

"Look, you haven't had a decent night's sleep in days. Get some shut-eye, and I'll take the wheel. Besides, I'm the one who can navigate the streets of L.A."

Sovo didn't seem to be a fan of gridlock, so he acquiesced quickly. We helped Destiny into the back, turned on the VCR for her and plugged in a Disney video, *Cinderella.* I rolled my eyes.

"How come you roll your eyes?" Sovo asked.

"All that Prince Charming crap."

He looked confused. I said, "Look, I like a good fairy tale as much as the next little girl, but I was raised without a whole lot of pixie dust. A very gritty world. Everyone in it pulls himself up by his bootstraps, by being tough, not by waiting for a guy with a crown to come fix everything."

Pulling away from the curb, I headed for the highway, knowing traffic would make all our lives miserable until we were out of L.A.

"It's going to be good to get home."

Sovo nodded.

"Go to sleep, Sovo."

Soon, he was dozing and I eased into bumper-to-bumper traffic. I checked my rearview mirror out of habit and saw two black Mercedes sedans with tinted windows and Nevada plates.

"Keep it together, Jack," I said to myself. I assumed it could be coincidence. Putting on my blinker, I switched lanes. So did they, albeit twenty cars back.

"Sovo…" I tapped his arm. "I think we're being followed."

He looked in the sideview mirror and concurred.

"How the fuck are they tracking us?" I grabbed my cell phone and speed-dialed Deacon.

"Where have you been, child?" he snapped at me.

"What are you talking about?"

"You still in the van?"

"Yeah, why?"

"I left a message for you at the hotel."

"We must have checked out. I didn't get it."

"Then I called your cell."

"I had it on vibrate while Destiny was sleeping. I must not have heard it. What's up?"

"Your van is low-jacked."

"What?"

"Jimenez. The traitor set you up. They have a satellite of wherever you're going, Jack."

"Goddamn them. I have to dump the van."

"No kidding. And do it fast."

"I will. As soon as I figure out how."

I felt a rush of panic roll through me.

"Hold on, guys."

I moved into the right lane, then drove onto the shoulder, driving fast up to the exit. I could see the two Mercedes making their move, but cars weren't letting them move over. Amen for rude drivers!

At the exit, I ran a red light. I drove through another red light and made a right, flying fast through a residential neighborhood. Finding a house that looked as if the owners were gone for the day, I abandoned the van, made a mental note of the address and then told Sovo and Destiny we had to travel lighter.

"Can I bring my backpack?" Destiny asked.

"Sure thing, sweetie," I said. I knew it contained her Barbies and things her mother had given her. She could have the pink backpack. Sovo and I each donned a jacket and strapped a gun into each holster. He handed me a knife, which I put in a sheath I tied around my calf. We combined a change of clothes each into a single duffel bag, and threw the tapes in there.

I looked at Sovo. "We passed a coffee shop two blocks back. One of those soy latte fat-free bullshit places. We abandon the van here, they'll find it, and think we're in the back. That'll buy us a little time. When they discover it's empty, logically, they'll think we went that way." I pointed to a side street. "But we're going this way, through a couple of backyards, to the coffee shop. From there, we get a cab to the airport."

"The airport?"

"Look, we can't fly home with all these weapons. And if they have Dillard on their team, he could easily search flight records, I would think. But there are a ton of car-rental places at the airport. We rent the most innocuous vehicle and we head home. If they stumble on us, or we're cornered in any way, you take Destiny."

"No, you. I distract them."

"Sovo, you can protect her better than I can. It's only a matter of time before they figure out we found the tapes. They want me. Not you, not her. They want the tapes. All we have to do is stay alive until Rob can set up a meeting with the FBI."

Hurriedly, we set out to cross through the neighborhood and backtracked to the coffee shop. I ran up front, carrying the duffel bag, Sovo followed with Destiny on his back.

"Hey you! Get out of my yard!" a woman yelled, while pruning her rosebush. "Don't step on my flowers!"

Christ, could she make any more noise? I looked behind me, and in the distance, I saw men in dark suits.

"Sovo!" I yelled. "They're on to us."

In one swift motion, he pulled Destiny from his back and handed her to me. Looking me deep in the eyes, he said, "Go. I hold them off."

"They'll kill you!"

"Not me. See you back at the ranch. Go!" He gave me a fast kiss for luck, and pulled his gun out and adopted a shooting stance.

Sweat poured down my face as I ran harder, carrying Destiny piggyback-style and managing not to drop the duffel bag. I heard a single shot ring out and looked back. Sovo was still standing, and one of the bad guys had fallen. I ran harder, my lungs feeling as if they would burst. I could see the coffee shop.

I ran up the street until I was safe inside the shop's doors. The place was packed. People in L.A. take their lattes seriously, I guess. I took Destiny into the ladies' room, and we stayed there fifteen minutes. I washed my face with cold water and called information, got the name of a cab company, and asked for a cab to pick us up at the coffee shop. I inhaled deeply several times. Destiny looked frightened. I knelt on the floor so we were eye level.

"We're going back to the ranch, Destiny. We're going to be fine."

"What about Sovo?"

My voice trembled. "He's fine. I have to believe he's fine, Destiny. He's a real soldier, and he knew what he was doing. Okay?"

Cautiously, I opened the door to the rest room. The coffee shop was still crowded, and I saw no men in dark suits on the sidewalk outside. We emerged from the bathroom, and went and sat on a cushioned leather bench to watch for the cab. About ten minutes later, a cab pulled up. Looking cautiously in all directions, I went out to it and shepherded Destiny into the back.

Exhaling, I said, "LAX, please. Hertz rental."

The cabbie nodded, and we were on our way. As we passed the side street near where we had parked the van, I looked in vain for Sovo. Holding Destiny's hand, I looked out the window and felt a tear wind its way down my face.

Chapter 15

Hertz was able to rent me a minivan. With a DVD player and VCR. I was grateful. With only me driving, Destiny would have to amuse herself for long hours without Sovo there to play Go Fish and Old Maid.

The minivan wasn't as spacious as the van we had, but it would do. I drove out of LAX and onto the highway and then started my trip toward Nevada. Toward home.

When I was about fifty miles from L.A., I pulled onto the shoulder and called Sovo's cell phone number. There was no answer. Then I tried calling Deacon.

"I got your package, child."

"Have you watched them yet?"

"Yes, I have. We're waiting on Rob to make arrangements with the FBI to hand over the tapes and the copies."

"I can't wait for this all to be over. Deacon?"

"Yes?"

"Have you heard from Sovo?"

"He's not with you?"

"No." I felt my voice crack. "Two Mercedes full of the big beefy types followed us. We had to abandon the van, anyway, so we took off on foot. I ran on with Destiny…and I don't know what happened to him."

"Believe me, it will take more than some big dumb lugs to get rid of Sovo."

"You're just being hopeful."

"Jack, I have faith. You know me. I always have faith."

"Call me if he turns up."

"Of course I will. Now, you keep focused on the drive, and on keeping that child safe."

"I will."

I drove until I thought I would pass out. After I found a hotel, I did exactly what Sovo did. I settled Destiny into the bed farthest from the door, and I slept with the gun under my pillow. I kept to myself, didn't ask questions and quietly ordered room service.

Sleep eluded me. I had been so tired on the road,

I had been nodding off, but in bed, I heard every noise. I heard the air conditioner turn on and footsteps in the hall. The ice maker was across the hall, and it made a lot of noise. But it wasn't just the noise. Mostly, for the first time in a long, long while, I said prayers that Sovo, Rob, Big Jimmy and Deacon were all safe. My mind went round and round with anxiety and prayers.

"Auntie Jack…are you awake?"

I almost forgot where I was. "Mmm-hmm," I mumbled.

"Wake up. We have to get home to Big Jimmy. We have to find Sovo."

As soon as she said that, it all came flooding back to me. I sat up and pulled Destiny to me. "Okay, kiddo."

We climbed out of bed and packed our now-meager belongings.

"We'll pick up McDonald's," I said.

"I want chicken nuggets."

I looked at my watch. "It's seven o'clock in the morning. You'll have to settle for an Egg McMuffin."

She screwed up her face.

"Pancakes?"

She brightened at that. "But I bet they won't be as good as Rob's or Mommy's."

"True enough."

We left the hotel, settled into the minivan and took to the highway after a brief stop at McDonald's. I was so sick of moving. I wanted to be in one place for a change. My ass was numb from all the driving, and I was bored out of my mind. I missed having Sovo for company, and every time I thought of that, I felt sick to my stomach.

When I was about two hours from home, I called Sovo's cell phone again. To my total shock, he answered.

"Oh, my God! Are you all right?"

"I'm okay."

"What happened?"

"You go first."

I told him about running with Destiny to the coffee place, going to LAX and renting the car. I let him know everyone got their packages, according to Deacon.

"And you. Please tell me you're totally fine."

"I'm, as you Americans say, A-OK. I shoot two bad guys. There were four of them."

"Did you—" I thought about Destiny in the back seat "—k-i-l-l them?"

"No. Wounded pretty bad. One guy takes bullet in his thigh. The other in the shoulder."

"And the other two?"

"Funny thing. They see their comrades fall. They run."

"That's what happens with hired guns."

"What do you mean?"

"Well, we protected Destiny because we care about her, not because someone is signing our paycheck. Are you okay? No bullet holes?"

"I was grazed. My arm. It's okay."

"I'll be the judge of that when I see you. Damn. Where are you?"

"I rented a car. I'm on my way home—back to the ranch. I should be there in a few hours."

"See you there. I'm two hours from home."

I drove the rest of the way, elated. I was so elated that I even allowed Destiny to hand me this children's sing-along tape, and she and I sang at the top of our lungs.

When the tape was over, I told her she couldn't tell anyone I was singing.

"Why?"

"It would ruin my reputation."

"Why?"

"Because I'm making a name for myself in a man's business. I have to watch out that no one thinks I'm too soft."

"Why?"

"Anyone ever tell you that you ask a lot of 'why' questions?"

"Yes. My mommy used to tell me that."

In a lot of ways, Destiny reminded me of myself when I was a little girl. She had so easily gone along with Sovo and me, adapting to each new situation. She was a kid with a lot of heart, but I worried she had been adapting *too* well. I longed for her and Big Jimmy to settle into a seminormal life. I wanted us all to go on.

When I arrived back at the ranch, I beeped my horn loudly and everyone came running out.

I opened the driver's side door, and Destiny climbed over into the front seat and I helped her out. Deacon reached us first, embracing me with a huge hug and lifting Destiny up.

"Hello, little angel. It's good to see you. We have a whole mess of chicken nuggets waiting for you. And a cake."

Eddie the Geek came forward with a new Barbie doll. I did a double take and blinked hard. Barbie was dressed in gym shorts and a T-shirt—and she had her hands taped.

"It's Boxing Barbie," he offered.

"They make one of those?"

"No. I improvised."

Destiny clutched the doll to her chest.

Standing in a big group a few steps back was Big Jimmy and his crew. These guys were built like double-wide trailers—huge barrel chests. They all had tattoos, a couple had earrings. They wore faded Levi's and biker boots. But they all were beaming like kindergarten teachers at the sight of Destiny. Deacon put her down gently and she tore away from us and ran over to Big Jimmy, who scooped her up as if she was a little doll and clutched her to his chest. She nuzzled him and nestled against him.

"I just want a hot shower and to be home," I said.

We all turned to walk inside. Deacon fell in step with me.

"Jimenez is gone?" I asked.

"Packed up yesterday. He was sniveling and crying. Miguel could have gotten you killed."

"And Terry? How's his training going?"

"Not as well as before."

"Why?"

"Two things. One, all this tension has been distracting, not the least of which is his own guilt. And two, frankly, his best sparring partner is Sovo. When Terry fights against Sovo, he has to rise to the occasion. Sovo thinks about every punch, almost as if he's studied everything there is to study about Terry. So when Terry drops his left shoulder to work his left hook, Sovo spots that and defends against that perfectly. Without Sovo here, Terry's a sloppier fighter."

"Sovo will be back today. He was just a few hours behind me."

"Good. I'd like for life to get back to normal. In the midst of all of this, I'm fielding calls from the media left and right. The hype for the fight is building."

We walked into the ranch house, and I headed back to my bedroom. "I'm going to shower and change. I had to ditch all my clothes in L.A."

Big Jimmy and Destiny went into the kitchen. Deacon and everyone else, too.

In my bedroom, I stripped out of my clothes, taking off the gun Sovo gave me and the knife on my leg. I had gotten so used to them, and until I met with the FBI, turned over the tapes, and was sure we were all going to be okay, I decided to keep them on me.

I walked into the bathroom off of my bedroom and started a hot, steamy shower. I climbed in and rinsed off the tension from the road. I was alone, and there, in the privacy of the shower stall, I allowed myself to cry.

I pulled myself together as I dried off. It was all going to be over soon, I hoped.

"Terry, come on, move away from the ropes. You're getting too tied up over there. This isn't wrestling."

Destiny was taking a nap, with Big Jimmy in a chair right next to the bed. I don't think he ever planned to let her out of his sight again. I was out in the barn, watching Terry spar. It was the worst I had ever seen him fight.

"Stay focused, Terry!"

Part of me wondered whether or not he might still be contemplating taking a dive. Why else was he so out of sorts?

"Stop with the clinches! Jesus, he gives you an uppercut in the clinch and you could end up in trouble."

Terry moved back and start bouncing from foot to foot, shaking his head, trying to get his concentration back. But again, he ended up in a clinch.

"Terry! Come on, damn you! Jake Johnson isn't some kid starting out. You're not going to be able to get away with a lazy fight."

At the word "lazy," Terry seemed to get annoyed and started fighting a little more like I wanted him to. But I was concerned. Christmas was around the corner. Then New Year's Eve. The fight for all the marbles.

"Okay, Terry, go shower. We'll view fight films tonight in the den."

Everyone else was back in the house, and I set about turning off all the lights. I heard someone come into the barn and turned and saw Sovo standing there looking tired but none the worse for wear.

"God, but you're a sight for sore eyes," I said, and smiled. I ran over to him and gave him a huge hug, avoiding the bandage on his upper arm.

He was so much taller than I that he had to sort of lean down to hug me. "Good to be back," he said.

I stepped away from him and took a good look at his face. He had circles under his eyes, and he was pale, but overall he seemed in good shape. A few days of rest and relaxation would do wonders.

"Why are you staring at me?" he asked.

"Just making sure you have no life-threatening injuries," I joked. "You look like you're all in one piece."

He patted his chest. "One piece."

We were standing there talking when the door opened. Rob came in—and looked none too pleased that I was alone with Sovo in the nearly dark barn.

"What's up, Jack?" he asked. But his smile was frozen on his face, and it certainly didn't travel to his eyes.

"Hi, Rob," I said a little awkwardly, and walked over to give him a hug.

Sovo nodded in our direction. "I'm going to the house." He turned and left without looking back.

"What's going on with you two?" Rob asked accusingly.

"What, no 'how are you after your extended road trip trying to stay alive'?"

"Well, that, first."

"I'm mentally and physically exhausted. I've got a heavyweight fighter who's boxing sloppy, his best sparring partner has a bullet wound on his arm, and I have in my possession a bunch of tapes that people would kill for—and have already killed for. I can't go to the police because the chief is implicated on the tapes, and so I have to rely on some nefarious meeting with the FBI and hope the feds don't screw this up royally and I don't end up dead like my friend Crystal. Other than that? I'm just peachy."

"Jack...have you ever thought of getting out of boxing? This whole thing is just a mess of trouble, and what's to say a year from now or two years from now, you won't run into a similar situation. Next time maybe the Mob will arrive at your doorstep."

"I have trouble believing the Mob would be *worse* than the guys chasing me now. Besides, I'm a boxing trainer and manager. It's what I do. More than that, it's who I am."

"Bullshit. You're a lot of things: beautiful, exasperating, stubborn, sexy, smart, resilient, and you have a decent left hook. But you don't have to swim in the cesspool of boxing just because you think that's who you are."

"Rob, this is the same argument we always have."

"I just want to marry you and ride off in the sunset—out of Las Vegas, to someplace far, far away from the thugs running the boxing industry."

"Okay, look, Prince Charming, I'm not looking for a rescue from boxing. I just want my father released and Perrone and Bonita to have side-by-side jail cells."

"Me, too. Now answer my question, Jack."

"What question?"

"What's with you and the Kosovo guy?"

"You know, I'm not even going to dignify that with an answer."

He shook his head, then seemed to come to his senses. "Sorry. It was just making me a little nuts having you on the road with that guy."

"It's okay. We're all under a lot of strain."

"Let's go back to the ranch."

"Sounds good."

"I got the tapes. How many copies did you say you made?"

"Three, plus the originals. Deacon has one set, Big Jimmy the second, you got yours today, and I kept the originals."

"When we meet with the FBI, we should have all the copies and the originals."

"What if something goes wrong? Those tapes are the only proof I have of who murdered Crystal."

"All the more reason to make sure they're all with the FBI. I don't want someone breaking in here and getting his hands on them."

I nodded. "How soon until we meet with the FBI?"

"I'm working on it."

We left the barn, and I locked it behind me. As we walked back to the ranch house, dusk had overtaken the sky and I could see a smattering of stars. I looked up, picked the first one I saw and made a wish.

Please protect us.

Chapter 16

While we waited for Rob to make arrangements regarding the tapes, and watched as former Hell's Angels circled the ranch on motorcycles and foot patrols, we planned for Christmas. We wanted Destiny to have everything she wished for. In my heart, I knew the *one* thing she wanted most, she couldn't have: her mother.

Still, we bought Barbies and a little tea set, and games like Candyland—because we'd *all* had enough with Go Fish. Sovo bought her a gold locket so she could wear a picture of her mother around her neck, and Big Jimmy bought her a beautiful wooden toy chest and had her name engraved on top.

Every day, we heard more and more questions about Santa. Would he really come? How did his reindeer fly so far in one night? And we all also received instructions.

"Now, Uncle Deacon, you cannot build a fire on Christmas Eve," she scolded us.

"But what if I'm cold?" he teased her.

"Still no fire. He has to come down the chimney."

Then she furrowed her brow and appeared to think of something very important. "Do you think Santa Claus will know to come here? Won't he be confused if I'm not at Uncle Tony's house?"

I remembered a boxing match that took place in Madison Square Garden in New York City near Christmas when I was about six. I was panicked that Santa would not be able to come to my hotel room. But Dad and Deacon had splurged for a small suite and bought a tabletop Christmas tree, and when I awoke Christmas morning, all my presents were there.

"Santa sees all, knows all. Trust me, he'll find you. But if it would make you feel better, we can write him a postcard and tell him your new address."

"Okay."

I hadn't planned on her saying yes, so we went to the office and dug out a blank piece of paper and an envelope.

"Sorry, kiddo, no postcards. Will a letter do?"

"Oh sure, Auntie Jack, a letter is better."

I wrote while she dictated.

Dear Santa,
I have been a very good girl this year. I listened
to my mommy and to Auntie Jack and Sovo
and Big Jimmy and Uncle Deacon. I am very
sad this year because I miss my mommy. If you
see her, tell her I said hello. I don't live at
Uncle Tony's house anymore, so you can find
me at Auntie Jack's ranch.
Love, Destiny

"Aren't you going to tell him what you want for
Christmas?"

She shook her head and sighed. "It really won't
be the same for Christmas this year."

"I know, honey. But I promise we'll still try to
make it special. It will be really different, but we'll
all do our best, okay?"

"Okay."

On Christmas Eve, Rob came to spend the night at
the ranch, and to tell me that Esposito's death had
been ruled a suicide. We sat outside on the porch away
from everyone so we could discuss things in private.

"Esposito, ten minutes after laying eyes on me,
decides to blow his brains out? Sure. What a joke. I
mean didn't they get any prints off the gun?"

"No one's but his. They also discovered a small
vault in his office, hidden in a coat closet. They found
Crystal's will."

"And?"

"It says for sure that Big Jimmy is the father, and she wants Destiny raised by him. You're executor of her estate. The coroner released her body to Perrone, before we found the will. He cremated her."

"Those ashes belong to her daughter."

"I know. That's something we'll straighten out, Jack."

"And what about her death? Are you all still working the junkie angle?"

"The toxicology reports aren't in yet. But there was heroin in the needle."

"I don't care if they found pure gold in her veins, she didn't do drugs. Period. They're just sweeping this away as if she never existed."

"Hang tight. The FBI can look into that, too."

"When?"

"Day after Christmas. We'll be dealing with an agent named Mark Spencer, who's from the field office for this area. My friend Steve Greene assigned it to this guy."

"As Deacon would say, amen and praise the Lord."

"Did you know you were executor of her estate?"

"What estate? She lived with Perrone."

"Yeah, but apparently she'd been socking away her paychecks from the show. I mean, he gave her credit cards to every high-end store in town, she had a car, spending money, clothes, jewelry. Destiny is actually a wealthy little girl."

"Really?"

"Yup. Big Jimmy and her could buy a ranch as big as this one if they wanted. She also has a trust fund for college that Perrone apparently set up."

"Wow! I never would have guessed it."

"What?"

"You know, that Crystal would be so responsible with her money."

"She sure as hell was. She also, according to the stock certificates in her name, invested wisely. She may have been a platinum blonde but no one was pulling any fast ones on her."

"So tell me about this FBI agent."

"Steve says he trusts Spencer. I talked to Spencer and he says he wants all the tapes, and he wants to talk to you, to see if you'd testify and so on. He'll take a statement, and then he'll start really pursuing the case."

"How soon do you think they'll get my father out?"

"That may be a little tricky. See, it's not a question of the FBI doing something. They have to go to a judge and ask him to release him or grant him a new trial."

I felt my heart sink somewhere down by my shoes. "I just figured that…you know, they'd let him go right away."

"That can happen. It can. Don't lose hope. We just have to see what we can get out of the deal."

I nodded, feeling a burning in my throat as emotions bubbled inside of me. I decided I would try to put it all aside and enjoy Christmas morning with Destiny. Then hopefully next year, I would celebrate with my father by my side.

She woke me and Rob up at five-thirty in the morning.

"Go back to sleep," I begged, rolling over and covering my head with a pillow.

"Please, Auntie Jack. Pl-ee-ee-ease." She said the second "please" as if it had four syllables, all capped with a whine.

I rolled over and looked at her little face, there pleading in the glow from the night-light.

"You realize you're going to make everyone crabby by getting us up this early."

"But we all have to see what Santa brought us."

"All right, all right." I rolled over to face Rob and poked him. "Kiddo here wants to see if Santa came."

He groaned, but not nearly as loud as the rest of the house as we went from room to room waking everyone. I sent Destiny in so that way they wouldn't yell at me. No one had the heart to turn down Destiny, and by ten minutes after six, we were sitting in the den, gathered around the tree, sipping *strong* coffee prepared by Eddie.

The adults each had two or three gifts under the tree. I bought Big Jimmy a print by a Native American painter he admired. I got Rob a sports jersey from his alma mater, and a series of books by his favorite author—Hemingway. I got Uncle Deacon a cool gadget that had the entire Bible Concordia listed. All he had to do was type in a word, like *faith*, and all the sentences with that word in it in the New Testament came up on the small screen and he could scroll until one struck his fancy.

Nervously, I watched Sovo open his gift. His eyes welled for a minute. He had told me once that his mother used to make a jam with wild blackberries. I found a place online that made it from scratch, and I got him a case of jam, as well as a DVD of his favorite movie—*High Noon*. It's an old movie and Gary Cooper portrayed someone not unlike Sovo, a little taciturn but willing to do the right thing.

Deacon and I chipped in and bought Terry a coffee-table book about Ali, his idol, as well as a poster from one of Ali's fights.

I gave Eddie a couple of DVDs of John Wayne movies. His favorite.

As for me, Rob got me perfume and a pair of diamond solitaire earrings; Deacon got me a beautiful new leather jacket for chilly Nevada nights in the desert; Terry and Eddie chipped in on a beautiful hand-carved teak box for the top of my dresser with my initials on it; and Sovo got me an antique jeweled picture frame. Big Jimmy and Destiny gave me a silver picture frame with "Auntie Jack" engraved on it and a picture of Destiny in it.

However, none of these presents compared to the explosion of gifts under the tree for Destiny. She squealed as she opened each one from Santa, and she came and gave a kiss to each of us as she opened our gifts to her. I think her favorite gifts were the locket from Sovo and the toy chest from Big Jimmy. She also liked mine and Deacon's gift. We had a warm-up jacket specially made for her that read Rooney Brothers Training Camp on the back.

"See Destiny?" I told her. "You're one of us now."

She tried it on immediately and wouldn't take it off all day—she even slept in it.

Later that night, after we drank the last of the eggnog and got sleepy from the big turkey Deacon cooked, I lay in bed watching Destiny as she slept. Rob had gone back into Vegas and told me to meet him at his apartment in the morning. Apparently the FBI agent wanted some clandestine meeting, so I would be going to another location, as yet unde-cided, a place where the agent was sure we couldn't be bugged.

I was anxious and tossed and turned. When I would gaze over at Destiny in a sound sleep, she looked so innocent. None of us could ever replace what she lost, but I knew we were all determined to. And the first step in that direction was to get the FBI to take down Tony Perrone and Benny Bonita.

Chapter 17

The next day, I sent Destiny off with Big Jimmy to play. Then I started getting ready to meet Rob. My door was ajar, and Sovo knocked on it.

"You going to meet the FBI agent?"

I nodded. Rob had called earlier and said to go directly to the meeting place instead of his apartment.

"Where's your gun?"

"My gun? I hope my shooting days are over, Sovo."

"No. Wear the gun and the knife."

"Why?"

"Because what if you are followed on the road?"

"Rob mapped out a route that backs around and

loops a few times. If I am followed, I'm pretty sure I'd lose them."

"And what if they storm into the meeting and you have no weapon?"

"I guess I'll cross that bridge when I get to it."

He shook his head. "No. For me? Wear the gun."

I looked up at his face. He meant every word of what he said.

"Okay, Sovo. I'll wear the gun."

I put on the holster and took the gun I was most familiar with. I strapped on the knife, and put on my new leather jacket.

"I follow you."

"Oh, no. Rob will be there."

"Where? Show me on a map."

"It's this place in downtown Vegas. A warehouse." I wrote down the address on the back of one of my business cards and handed it to him.

"Trust me on this one. Today is the day we can all relax. The tapes will be turned over to the feds and our lives will get back to normal."

"Hope so," Sovo said. He tucked the card into his pocket and left the room.

I took a small gym bag and put the tapes in—the originals, Deacon's and Big Jimmy's. Rob was bringing his. But suddenly, I thought that maybe I should still keep the originals. I wanted to make sure I liked what the FBI had to say.

I went out into the den. Deacon lived for TiVo, so we didn't put much on videocassette, but we had half a dozen blank ones to tape movies we liked and wanted to keep. I grabbed three blanks and walked back to my room. I took the originals out of my bag and hid them under my mattress. Then I thought better of the idea—the mattress is the first place a bad guy looks, I reasoned.

I walked down the hall to the office, which was empty. In the office is a long leather couch, and the back of the couch is against the far wall. The reason this particular leather couch was regulated to a wall had as much to do with practicality as interior design.

One day, maybe a year before, one of our boxers had gotten good and drunk while watching a pay-per-view fight with us in the den—the former home of the couch. There was a bad decision. In boxing, you can knock out your opponent, meaning you hit him until he's unconscious and can't get up by the count of ten; you can get a technical knockout, for instance, depending on the rules of the bout, which vary from state to state and venue to venue; or you can get a decision, in which the judges watching the boxing match award points based on aggressiveness, punches landed, and so on. Not everyone agrees with the judges, who often favor a champ over an up-and-comer, even if the new guy is really the better boxer. Anyway, this boxer was so drunk, and so mad over the decision, that he kicked the back of the leather sofa and put a nice hole in it. We had to move the couch. Deacon wanted to pitch it because he's meticulous about his house, but I voted to keep it and put it against the wall in the den so you couldn't see the hole.

I pulled the couch out from the wall and put the three tapes into the hole. So while it wasn't as good as a safe, I doubted anyone would find them. I felt better having hid them there. But something about Sovo's cautious behavior made me nervous. I wondered if snipers have a sixth sense when it comes to things going down.

I sure as hell hoped not.

"Jesus Christ," I said aloud to myself as I drove to the meeting spot. "Could the FBI pick a skuzzier place for this meeting?"

I parked my car, certain all my hubcaps would be stolen by the time I got out of my meeting, but I just wanted the damn thing over with, and if I lost a few hubcaps in the process, so be it.

I strode into the warehouse projecting confidence I didn't exactly feel. Almost subconsciously, I patted my side and felt my gun.

"Hello? Rob?"

"Over here, baby."

I picked my way through boxes. The place smelled like motor oil and urine. I walked in the direction of Rob's voice and thankfully found him and a well-built man with close-cropped sandy blond hair sitting at a table. The lights were bright, and the floor was swept clean. I started to feel a little better.

Both men stood, and Rob gave me a peck on the cheek.

I turned slightly to face the agent head on. "Mark Spencer," the agent said, and stuck out his hand.

"Jackie Rooney. Everyone calls me Jack." He had a firm, cool handshake. Another good sign. And he looked self-assured.

"Have a seat."

The three of us sat on folding chairs, the metal cold to my touch as I put my hands down by my side.

"Rob has been doing a tremendous job filling me in on your ordeal."

"That's a good name for it. An ordeal."

"Well, we're happy that you've come forward with this information."

"Thanks. All I want is my old life back. It seems like everywhere I turned these last weeks, someone has either turned up dead, or men have been following me. Big, mean men, I might add."

Mark gave me a smile. "I can only imagine."

"All I want is to be left alone. I want Crystal's daughter left alone. I want to be able to exist without looking over my shoulder every five minutes."

"I understand, and that's why I'm here."

Rob leaned over and patted my hand. I felt all sorts of tension leave me. There was a light at the end of the tunnel.

"Now, what, specifically, is on these tapes?"

"They talk about having framed my father, organized crime, fixing boxing matches.... You name it, and Benny Bonita was into it. What amazes me is that Tony Perrone would risk so much when he already has zillions of dollars."

"I can tell you greed knows no boundaries. Even people who have it all—or at least look like they have it all—want more."

"I'm happy with my own little corner of the world. And I just want it back."

"Now, do you have all the copies of the tapes and the originals?"

I nodded, putting the nylon gym bag on the table. "Three originals and two copies of each set. Nine tapes."

"And that's all of them?"

I hesitated a second.

"All of them? This is all of them, right?"

I nodded. "Except for Rob's."

"I have those already." He opened the gym bag and counted the tapes. "Nine. Excellent. Which are the originals? In a court of law, the originals prove the tape wasn't altered in any fashion."

I stood and peered into the bag. "Um…I didn't label them. They're in there, though."

"All right. When we get back to the office, we'll be able to tell."

"So do you think you can clear my father based on what's on the tapes?"

He nodded. He had brown eyes and a strong nose and square chin.

"Are you sure?"

"Fairly confident. But I'll have to view them for myself first."

"Well, then, what's the next step?"

"I go back to the field office and examine these, and then we move to capture Perrone and Bonita."

"What about protection for me, my family, Destiny?"

He looked at Rob, who said, "I'll take care of that. Besides, this will go down soon."

"But why wouldn't the FBI assign some agents to us?"

Spencer said, "Manpower. The local police, Rob here, can cooperate with us and coordinate protection."

"He did tell you his boss is on the tape, right? The chief? I mean, I don't know if I want a bunch of cops around—no offense, Rob."

"None taken. We'll work something out," Rob said, and stood. "Come on, I'll walk you to your car."

"I don't know. It doesn't seem to go like this in the movies. I thought we'd go into witness security or something."

"That program is run through the federal marshals. And you have to…there are certain ways you qualify for that, and this likely wouldn't be one of those."

"Oh." I thought about it. "Because to me, Tony Perrone is just as dangerous as anybody in the Mob."

"Rob can handle security. I promise you'll be safe."

I stood and extended my hand to the FBI agent. Then I thought of something.

"Can I have one of your business cards?"

"Hmm?"

"A business card. In case we're threatened. I mean, Rob can't provide protection 24/7. And what if I can't get a hold of him?"

Mark Spencer looked at Rob. "I'm sorry. I'm out of cards at the moment."

A creepy chill came over me. Something wasn't right with this meeting. But my dad and Deacon taught me not to be afraid and to speak my mind. "You know, can I see your badge? Identification?" I looked over at Rob. "I mean, how do you know this guy is legit?"

I stepped back from the table. Mark Spencer was no longer smiling. In fact, he looked majorly pissed off.

"I want to see your badge, *dickhead,*" I said evenly.

"Being as this is undercover, I don't have any on me."

"This is bullshit. This smells wrong."

Suddenly Spencer grabbed the duffel bag.

"Whoa! Put them down, asshole."

"Look, I've got to go back to the office."

I opened my jacket and pulled out my gun. Taking two steps back, I trained it right at his chest. "Put…down…the tapes."

Rob started flipping out. "Jesus Christ, Jack, since when did you start carrying a gun?"

"Since my world became populated by assholes."

Spencer had frozen, but he had *not* dropped my tapes. Inwardly, I was grateful I had the originals. Rob had obviously been fooled by this guy.

"Jack," Rob soothed, "put down the gun. You can't go pulling guns on federal agents."

"No. I will not put it down, and this guy isn't a federal agent, Rob, come on. At least if you're going to pretend to be a fucking FBI agent, asshole, get a badge to flash. Make yourself look legit."

"Jack…hand me the gun," Rob commanded.

"Not until I get some answers. I want to see this guy's badge."

The agent wasn't making any move to get his wallet out of his pants pocket or out of his jacket. I pulled out my cell phone from my coat pocket with one hand and tossed it toward Mark Spencer—if that was even his real name.

"Go ahead. Punch in the phone number to the bureau. Ask for your secretary. Ask for your boss. Get the main switchboard. Something. Anything. Prove me wrong."

He stared at me with hatred in his eyes. Then he barked at Rob, "I thought you said she'd cooperate with this, man."

I felt like someone had punched me in my chest and knocked the wind out of me.

"Rob?" I took two more steps backward and trained the gun on both of them. Back and forth I moved from one to the other, feeling as if my whole world had just collapsed. "Rob? What's going on?"

"Jack, put down the gun. There's a logical explanation for all this."

My breath was coming in shallow gasps. My father had told me that in the ring, a man feels both fear and anger. He wants to destroy his opponent, but he also knows to do so, he risks destruction. I'd rather be angry than frightened. Moving closer to Spencer, I again repeated my instructions to drop the bag.

"No. Shoot me. You don't have the guts."

Rob said, "No, Jack. You have to trust me, baby. I'm getting us out of this jam."

"Back away, Rob, or I shoot him."

"You wouldn't."

"I wouldn't have three weeks ago, but now I would."

Spencer was watching me and Rob, looking to see how it would go down, I guess. While he wasn't expecting it, I took the barrel of my gun and struck Spencer in the temple. He fell like an accordion folding up on itself.

"And now," I said to Rob, "we see what kind of a mess you've gotten me into, Rob."

Chapter 18

I kept the gun trained on Rob, who repeated over and over that I had to trust him. He also tossed in, "You're crazy, Jack" and "The stress has gotten to you."

I had pistol-whipped Mark Spencer but good. He'd have a nice egg-size welt when he woke up. And a headache to match.

I opened his jacket and found his breast pocket. His wallet was in there.

"Let's see," I said, flipping the wallet open. "We have a Mr. John Tanner, who resides in Las Vegas…and no sign whatsoever that he's an officer of any kind."

"I had no idea, Jack. I was set up by my friend.

This was the guy he recommended. I had no reason to doubt him."

"What about when he said you told him I would cooperate."

"Well, I did. I told him you'd turn over the tapes, and you wanted your father released from prison. Put the gun down, Jack. I'm begging you. Take it from a cop, once you escalate to guns, the situation starts spinning out of control."

"So now we have a situation? I mean now that I realize I've been set up, nothing makes sense today. Why not meet at the FBI field office? Why this bad B-movie setup in a warehouse? No, none of this smells right, Rob, and you least of all."

And that was the last thing I said, because seconds later, someone sneaked up from behind me and smashed me on the head and the world went very, very dark.

I woke up in a strange room, pale light from dusk coming in through the windows. My head throbbed. It actually felt as if it had a heartbeat of its own. If I blinked, it hurt worse, so I closed my eyes for a few moments. Then I opened them again.

Blurrily, I saw that I was in a well-appointed room, which, as I found out when I rose from the bed and tried the handle of the door, was locked from the outside. A window told me it was nearing nightfall. I walked over to the window and saw I was three stories up. No escape through there unless I learned to fly like Superman. Or Wonder Woman. Or grew webs like Spider-Man.

My throat was parched. I wanted water. I wanted to be home. I wanted a hot shower. And more than anything, I wanted to go backward in time to when my father wasn't in prison and my boyfriend wasn't a bastard.

My jacket was draped over a chair. I patted my holster. My gun was gone. But, amazingly, they had missed the knife. So that was a little ray of sunshine, not that I had ever used a knife before. My cell phone was, of course, gone.

I sat on the bed again. Sovo must know I had been kidnapped. I felt a sense of gratefulness that he had asked me where I was going and had noted the address. And everyone back at the ranch would all have to be idiots not to know I was now in either Tony Perrone's house or Benny Bonita's house—or someplace affiliated with one or the other. I ran back to the window. The zoo in the distance told me I was in Perrone's house. Crystal's former house. I knew the place was fifteen thousand square feet of pure luxury. No matter, to me it was still a prison.

I heard someone fiddling with the lock, and I ran and flopped on the bed, feigning sleep. Someone had walked into the room, shutting the door behind him. I rolled over and opened my eyes, pretending to wake up from the noise. It was Rob.

"Get away from me," I snapped, quickly sitting up.

"No. Baby, I love you. I promise you this is all going to work out okay."

"How? You tell me how."

He sat on the bed. "Look, Tony wants to bring Bonita down. The tapes contain all the proof he needs. And he knows you kept the originals, Jack. We played all the tapes. Nine were perfect, and surprise! Three were blank tapes. So you've got to give them to him. Tony's not a bad guy. You'll get what you want—your father will be exonerated—and Benny Bonita will go down. I thought that was all you ever dreamed of."

"But not this way, Rob. Not cooperating with the man who killed Crystal."

"He said it was Bonita's men. He's grief-stricken."

"Boo-hoo, let me fucking cry for him. And what about the stuff on the tape that incriminates Perrone? And how did Bonita find out about the tapes if Perrone planned to use them to take him down? Perrone is lying to cover his own ass. He'll say *or do* anything to get those tapes back."

"Baby, come on. Don't be difficult. For once in your life, can't you just go along?"

"Don't call me 'baby.' Don't call me anything. You lost the right to any part of me the day you struck a deal with Perrone, whom I note you appear to be on a first-name basis with."

"I've known Tony a long time." He touched my thigh, and I pulled away. I was repulsed by him.

"What do you mean? How do you know him?"

"I mean I used to moonlight in security for him. We got to be friendly. Over time, I started doing him some favors. It was a way to earn money on the side, Jack. And when I wanted to make detective, he reciprocated by making sure I got that promotion."

"I think I'm going to be sick."

"Now, Jack, you're streetwise. Don't act all naive and Pollyanna-ish. Or worse, act all stuck up. Like you think you're too good for this. I wanted the good life for us. And when this whole thing with Bonita came up, fixing the fights, the consortium of investors, this was my big chance. I'll clear enough from this to support you in style."

"I'm not interested in being supported in style. I'm *happy* out at the ranch."

"Sure. With your precious Sovo."

"You're disgusting. Nothing happened between us."

"Look, I'll admit he's good-looking. Did you fuck him?"

"You're sick, Rob. He has nothing to do with this. This is about your moral compass losing its magnetic north."

"I know in time, you'll forgive me. We're meant to be together, Jack, and when you forgive me, we'll be rich. Your father will be free. Big Jimmy will have Destiny. It'll all work out just the way I planned it."

"Who murdered Crystal, really?"

"Bonita."

"And who killed Crystal's lawyer? Whoever it was ransacked his office looking for the tapes."

"The poor guy committed suicide." Rob looked at me, and his usually warm eyes were flat and cold, like a shark's.

"Get out."

"You're really not in a position to order me around. But, because I love you, I'll get out. I'll give you time to think it over. We're going to bring a phone in here later tonight, and you're going to call Deacon and tell him to bring the tapes."

"He doesn't know where they are. Please, leave my family out of this, Rob."

"See, I figured he didn't know anything about you switching the tapes with the blank ones. Clever. But it doesn't matter. We'll bring you the phone and you'll tell him where they are. In a way, *you* brought your family into this, not me."

"Fuck you."

"I'd love to, honey, but I have to go." Smirking, he stood and walked to the door. "Come to your senses, Jack. This is all for the best."

He shut the door, and I heard him locking the door from the outside. I felt sick from the likely concussion I had—and from the feeling that I had given my heart to a double-crossing, back-stabbing creep.

I stood and paced, my head still throbbing from the butt end of a gun. And also from the way my mind was spinning. My fiancé was a prick, pure and simple. I hated him the way I hated Benny Bonita. Suddenly, I really did feel like I was going to vomit, and I raced to the bathroom and leaned over the bowl. I tried to fight the panic that threatened to overtake me. Pins and needles tingled on the back of my neck.

I rubbed my hands together. They were ice-cold from the nerves and shock of the whole thing. I knew I had to get out of there. I ran the water in the sink as hot as it would go and rinsed my hands, and then took some water in my mouth to rinse the acrid taste.

Don't panic, Jack. Think like a sniper. What do you see? What did you observe?

I went over to the window. I assumed two things. Perrone was likely videotaping my room. And the window was wired for an alarm. An alarm! I looked up at the ceiling and, in the corner, I spied a smoke detector.

That gave me an idea. Just outside the window, there was a wrought-iron grill that held a flower box in place. Tulips bloomed like it was fucking Holland. I wondered if the metal grill would hold me. I sure as hell wasn't going to wait for them to kill me once they had what they wanted. I'd rather take my chances with the roof, I decided.

I looked at the flower box. If it, indeed, could hold me, I could use that to stand on and then pull myself up and crawl out onto the roof. If I set a fire, the smoke detector would probably, with Perrone's money, alert the fire department. When I opened the window, the security alarms would go off, and I assumed a man like Perrone had a system that alerted the police right away. He wouldn't have some alarm company only—no, he'd want the best. Even with Chief Dillard on the take, I'd take my chances with the police. So if I set off the alarm, when the police came, I would scream and yell from the roof to get their attention. Weak plan, but it was the best I could do. Then I decided to up the ante.

The bathroom. I went back in and looked in every drawer. I noticed a gorgeous candle on the countertop. Its wick had clearly been lit before. And where there are candles, there are often matches and lighters. I opened cabinets, which were empty, and then a drawer, quietly, and voilà…at the very back of the drawer was an old set of matches. I stuck them in my pocket and went back to the bedroom. I turned out the light and pretended I was going to sleep. I wanted them to think I was tired from the blow to my head. I lay perfectly still for two hours in the darkness while in my mind I rehearsed everything. It was a technique we used with our boxers—visualization. You visualize the perfect fight in your mind over and over and over again. You anticipate every punch; you see it all clear as day. I visualized escaping. I went through each step in my mind.

Finally, I rolled out of bed, keeping the blankets looking full. On my belly, "commando crawl" style, I went to the window again. Were Deacon, Sovo and

Big Jimmy already on their way? Should I risk my life if they were coming to get me?

I went back to the bedding and lit a match, holding it up to a corner of the sheet. If I got a good mattress fire going, I assumed the alarm would detect smoke and key into the fire department. Two teams of guys—one cops and the other fire rescue. Two chances to be seen and then plucked from the roof.

Smoke started filling the air. I remembered a bottle of hairspray in the bathroom and ran to get it. There were two. I read the labels. Alcohol. Bingo. I sprayed them on the mattress, lit more matches and went to the window and opened it up. An alarm didn't ring out, which didn't worry me. He'd have a silent alarm. I felt the flower box. It seemed strong enough. But I still needed to be able to hoist myself up onto the roof.

I stepped out into the flower box and stood on tiptoe trying to avoid looking down. My fingers just reached the gutter of the roof. I mentally thanked Deacon and my father for making me work out with heavy bags from the time I was a little girl. My upper arms show incredible definition and muscles. I told myself climbing on the roof was going to be like doing a pull-up.

Only I would die if I failed.

Nothing like a little pressure.

I shut the window to give myself even that extra second or so they would need to open it. Through the window, I saw men burst into the room at the moment the mattress started flaming. It was now or never so, using all my strength, I swung from side to side a bit, kicking my foot up to the roof and raising myself up at the same time. I grunted from the effort. It was agonizing. My arms felt like they were going to be pulled from the sockets, and my sore shoulder seemed to be saying, "Jack, what the *hell* do you think you're doing?"

On the roof, I caught my breath and listened for a moment. I was waiting for sirens. Creeping along the roof, I made it to one of several chimneys and clung to it. My arms hurt. Is there a stronger word than *hurt?* But I had no time to bitch or worry about it. I walked to the other side of the roof. There was a huge pool below. I wondered if I could take a running jump and land in it. Two men appeared on the lawn at the front of the house. They pointed at the roof and were shouting. One fired a gun. The bullet hit the chimney.

"Come on, police," I said under my breath. Smoke was billowing toward the sky from the now-open window of the bedroom where I had been held. Finally, I heard the blessed sirens. Three fire engines and two squad cars arrived—that was what Tony Perrone's power could buy. I stared down and saw Perrone walk toward the firefighters. This was my opportunity.

I went to face the pool. I had no time to reason myself out of it. Taking two steps back, I took a running leap and landed in the pool with a splash. The extra height meant when I landed, I sunk all the way to the bottom of the pool with the momentum of the leap. Pushing up with my feet, I burst to the top of the pool and gasped fresh air. Hurriedly, I made my way to the side and climbed out. Still no one came, thankfully. I raced over to the side of his lawn. There were brick walls all around his estate. But they weren't topped with razor wire or anything, so I decided to chance climbing a tree and hoisting myself over the fence. Twenty minutes before, I would have felt fearful it was too big a drop, but after my leap from the roof, everything and anything felt possible.

I climbed a tree, maneuvered out on a bough and onto the brick wall. Looking back at the house, I could see the fire trucks hadn't left yet, but two men were clearly searching for me on foot, their flashlight beams glowing in the dark. I heard dogs barking. Sounded like big, snarling dogs. The better to bite me with. I slipped over the wall and started running. It wasn't like I was going to find a cab in this area of the mega wealthy, not to mention I was soaking wet and my hair looked like a Chia Pet from the water.

I cut across the street and through a few yards as fast as I could. The night was crisp and cool, and I shivered a bit.

Finally, I came to a house—more of a mansion, really, with an imposing white front with Georgian columns—where two people were climbing out of a Jaguar.

"Excuse me," I said, out of breath and leaning over a bit, my chest heaving.

They both startled, and the wife, dressed in what looked like designer duds from head to toe, looked at me in my pathetic water-rat imitation. She looked as if she was staring at something repugnant. Yeah, well, I forgot my dress clothes, what can I say?

"Yes," the husband said warily.

"I'm sorry to bother you. I'm sorry to frighten you. Uh, but I…um…Tony Perrone's house had a small fire tonight, and the firefighters were there and so on, and I got soaked. I need to call my uncle to come pick me up. Can I use your cell phone? I will gladly pay for the call."

The wife said, "I don't think so. Honey, call the police."

The man looked at me suspiciously. "So why wouldn't you call from Mr. Perrone's estate?"

Because he kidnapped me. But I didn't see the point in going into it. No, that was the final straw at the end of a long day and night. I bent over, lifted up my pant leg, and stood, holding the knife in front of me. "Don't make me have to hurt you. Give me the fucking phone for two minutes and I'll happily promise to never see either of you again."

The husband obliged while his wife still looked as if a large stick had been inserted up her ass.

I dialed Deacon's number.

"Deacon…Rob's a traitor."

"What?"

"He's been working for Perrone. He set me up today. There was no FBI agent. I'm just sick over it."

"Oh, sweet Jesus, Jack."

"I know!"

"No, honey…" His voice caught, and he stopped speaking for a moment.

"What is it?"

Still he couldn't speak. I heard him moan.

"Deacon! You're scaring me. Bad."

"Rob came out here about an hour ago. He said you were at his apartment and you had both decided Destiny would be safer away from the ranch."

"Oh, God, no!" My teeth began chattering from nerves.

"Jack…he has Destiny."

Chapter 19

I gave Deacon a cross street and took off on foot after handing the phone back to the husband and wife.

"Thank you," I whispered. "I'm sorry that I had to be so forceful. You just have to believe me when I say this was a matter of life or death."

The husband looked me in the eye as I put away my knife. He seemed to believe me. I took off and ran in the opposite direction. I stood behind some hedges at the street where I told Deacon to get me and waited. Sovo turned up in Deacon's Lexus. I jogged over to the car and climbed into the passenger seat. At the sight of a friendly face, I welled up.

"Don't cry," Sovo said. "Get even."

I wiped at my face and nodded. "That bastard will live to regret the day when he took that child."

Sovo sped away. "If he harms one hair on her head, I kill him."

"Get in line, buddy," I said. "Get in line."

We drove through the night back to the ranch. I thought back over all the times I had made love to Rob, all the times I had been vulnerable and had shared with him my fears about my father dying in prison, or about how it wasn't always easy being the only motherless girl at the Sacred Heart Academy where Dad and Deacon sent me to school. I thought of happy times when we'd all gathered together for a meal, about the way Deacon would always wrap an arm around Rob's shoulder and the way he called him "son." How could he be so misguided? How had I been so deceived?

Sovo kept glancing over at me. "What are you thinking?"

"First, how I was betrayed. Second, how I will get even."

"We'll get her back."

"How?"

"We give them what they want. We make a trade."

"But that won't be the end of it, Sovo. We're witnesses to what they've done. We give them what they want, and they simply kill us."

"Then we take her. Commando-style."

"Now we're talking."

A short while later, we arrived at the ranch. If I was a wreck about Destiny, I could only imagine how Big Jimmy was.

Deacon came out to the car. "You look terrible, Jack."

"Thanks. It's a combination of a clunk on the head, a jump from a roof and assorted other fiascos."

I climbed out of the car and shivered.

"Come on inside."

"Where's Big Jimmy?"

"He's in bad shape. He's locked himself out in the barn."

"Have you talked to him?"

"He won't listen. He won't come out."

"Let me go talk to him."

"Why don't we take a look at your head first, and then you go try to talk."

Reluctantly, I agreed. Deacon and Sovo escorted me into the house, and Terry and Eddie were in the den, pacing. Both of them came over and hugged me, patting me on the back.

We went into the kitchen, and Deacon sat me down and lifted up my hair, touching the nape of my neck, where I'd sustained the blow. It hurt like hell.

"They meant business," my uncle said.

"I know. I'm the one with the headache, Deacon."

"I'll fix you an ice pack. Go shower. You'll feel better. Your skin is clammy and cold. No sense you getting sick. You can't help Destiny if you're sick. There's dried blood on the back of your head, too."

He leaned in closer. "But the bleeding's stopped. Still, you need a hot shower."

I knew he was right. I couldn't help her if I was in shock or sick. I nodded at the guys and went to my room. Instantly, I missed her. God, how my life had changed. From never spending five minutes alone with a child to her being much of my waking thoughts. I lay down on the bed and put my head on her pillow. It smelled of baby shampoo, and I felt something between a stabbing and an ache in my heart.

Someone knocked on my door.

"Come in," I said listlessly.

Sovo walked into the room. We stared at each other, and he came and sat down. My face was still lying on Destiny's pillow.

"I have to say something," he said.

"Go ahead."

"We went on road…it was dangerous. I slept with guns again."

"I know."

"But I didn't mind. Because I was on the road with you."

I nodded. He lay down and faced me.

"I'm sorry about Rob."

"I don't know how he fooled us all."

"He fooled me, too. I told myself he was a better man for you."

I reached out with my hand and touched his cheek. "Remember when I said any woman would be a fool who didn't accept your past?"

He nodded.

"I meant it." Leaning in close, I kissed him on his cheek. "We'll figure it all out. Right now, we have a little girl to get home."

He hugged me, drawing me to him. My heart was pounding—and I felt more confused than ever.

"I better get in the shower and go out to see Big Jimmy." I sat up and walked into the bathroom. When I turned to shut the door, Sovo was holding Destiny's Barbie doll, the one Eddie the Geek made for her with boxing tape on her little plastic hands. His face set, almost like stone, Sovo turned and left my room.

The warm shower felt good. I scrubbed as gently as I could the spot where I'd been pistol-whipped. When I stepped out from the shower, I was still chilled to the bone. If things weren't so crazy, I would have slid under four blankets and gone to sleep for a long while. But that wasn't an option. Instead, I donned a pair of Levi's, a warm black turtleneck and a bomber jacket. Then I walked through the house and told Deacon I was going to the barn.

I reached the large doors to our training facility and knocked.

"Go away!" Big Jimmy shouted.

"It's me, Jimmy," I said through the doors. "It's Jack. Let me in."

There was a long period of silence.

"I'm not going away. And everyone knows how stubborn I am."

I heard footsteps and fumbling with the lock. Big Jimmy opened the door and let me in. When he shut the door, the first thing I did was hug him. I could hear him stifle a sob, and then he cried. He needed to. First he lost Crystal, granted he had lost her years before, but now the love of his life was gone with no possibility of returning. The idea of also losing Destiny was just too much.

I patted his back and let him get out his emotions. Then I stepped away. "We're going to take her back again."

"If they hurt her in any way, if they frighten her, I'll kill them—Rob included. I don't care that he used to be one of us."

"Well, a line is forming around the block to kill these guys, so you'll have to wait your turn."

Big Jimmy sat down and put his head in his hands. "I'm not good with plans. I just react, you know. You need some muscle, you say, 'Jimmy, go put that guy in a headlock,' and I do it. But this whole thing of coming up with a plan, I'm no good at that, but I want to be part of it."

"Of course you do. And we need you. Look, Jimmy, Destiny is going to come home. I swear it."

He nodded and stood.

"Come on, big guy, let's go back to the house."

I slid my arm around his waist. "We'll need some more guns, by the way."

"You tell me what you want, I'll get them."

"Good."

"Can I tell you something?"

"Sure." We turned around and locked the door.

"Sovo was insane while you were missing."

"He's a good guy."

"Yeah. He's really one of us. And personally, I want to be there when he takes down Rob."

"Rob is mine. I want to take him down myself."

We sat at the kitchen table, drinking hot coffee and devising a rudimentary plan. Deacon and I would arrange a meeting to turn over the tapes, and Big Jimmy, his posse of motorcycle buddies and Sovo would lie in wait to take down the bad guys. It was understood that only when Destiny was safe would we begin shooting. We all understood that until we figured out where the chain of corruption ended, there was no way we could bring in the authorities. We were completely and totally on our own.

"So where do we set up the meeting?" Terry asked. I wasn't thrilled with him being so distracted so close to the fight. I also didn't want him injured.

"Terry, maybe you should stay here. Be our point person at the ranch."

"Not a chance. That kid belongs to all of us. I'm in. So where do we meet them?"

"Well, we may not have a choice," I said. "They could demand I come to them with the tapes."

Sovo slammed his hand down on the table, shaking everyone's coffee mug. "No. You call them. You take charge. You be decisive." Then he looked at me. "You can make Rob believe you. Do it."

There was a small canyon off of a back road where Rob and I used to go hiking. He knew it, there was a gravel turnoff there, and better yet, it afforded numerous hiding places. We decided on that.

Deacon looked at me. "Jack, this is a giant game of chicken. You can't blink first. You have to tell yourself you're going to the mat on this one. It's like a boxing match. The last man standing wins. Knock-out."

"Right." I sipped my coffee, wondering if Rob was keeping Destiny at Perrone's house. Was she in her old room with her doll collection that she told me about? I prayed she didn't grasp what was going on.

Suddenly, my cell phone rang.

"Christ, this is it, boys."

Don't blink first, Jack. Last man standing wins.

"Hello?"

"Hello, my love," Rob said.

"You bastard!"

"I think I have something that belongs to Big Jimmy."

"And I think I have something that Perrone wants."

"Bonita wants it, too. How do I know you haven't cast your lot with him?"

"Because, unlike you, Rob, I wouldn't cast my lot with scum." I inhaled and tried to stay calm and focused. Everyone around the table was silent, but they all urged me on with their eyes.

"And how do I know you haven't made copies?"

In truth, Eddie had made copies, which were now safely locked in Deacon's safety deposit vault at the bank.

"Because these tapes have caused me nothing but headaches. I want them out of my hands. And if I had to choose one creep to bring down over another, trust me, Rob, you weren't wrong. I would rather bring down Bonita and see my father freed than say anything to anyone about Perrone. I want my old life back."

"Does that include me?"

Involuntarily, I ground my teeth. "Rob…" I led him on. "I know you meant to do the right thing, so maybe when all is over and done with, we can talk. Not right now. I'm still furious with you."

"Okay, baby."

"I want to meet at Rainbow Canyon."

"No can do, Jack. Tony wants a meeting here at his office. No guns. No one else. Just you and the tapes. You give us the original tapes, and we give you the girl. No hard feelings."

"Not a chance. First of all, the last time you picked the meeting place, I got a welt the size of a tangerine on the back of my head."

"I'm sorry. You just weren't being reasonable."

"It doesn't matter. There's only one road into the canyon. We meet at dusk. One car with Deacon and me, one for you and Tony. No cell phone signals can be picked up there. No guns. Just a meeting. An even trade."

"Not a chance."

"That's my final offer. And Rob, if Destiny is hurt in any way, there won't be a place on the goddamn planet where you can hide. I *will* kill you. And I won't even blink."

I closed my cell phone and ended the conversation. I figured he'd relay the offer to Perrone and come back with a counteroffer.

"You did good, Jack," Deacon said.

"Well, Perrone's obviously got ice water in his veins, Bonita's a hothead, Rob is clearly off the deep end, so I've got to call their bluff."

We all sat staring at the phone, willing it to ring. Fifteen minutes later, it did.

"Hello?"

"Perrone says no deal."

"Fine. I'll go to the real FBI. I don't give a shit, I just want Destiny back."

"So you'd risk Destiny's life?"

"So you'd risk yours? Because if she's harmed, I swear to you I will cut off your testicles and watch you bleed to death." I envisioned Rob's dick shrinking as I said it. Then I hung up the phone again.

"Harsh," Terry said.

"I meant it."

Five minutes later, Rob called back. "All right. You have a deal. Canyon. Tomorrow evening at six-thirty. No funny stuff."

"I see any bullshit, the deal's off."

I hung up the phone. "Well, guys, looks like we better prepare for a showdown."

Chapter 20

Logistics was Deacon's, Sovo's and my strong suit. Sovo had the background as a sniper, Deacon as a man who studied every move in a fight and how to react, and me the expert in visualization after following in Deacon's and my father's path. The fighter who doesn't plan his fight, who merely reacts to every punch thrown, will end up the loser. With so much at stake, we had to be the last man standing. Last woman standing.

We mapped out a plan, trying to envision every dirty trick, every eventuality. We talked until one o'clock in the morning, then we all went to bed. I'm not sure if any of us slept well. I put my head on Destiny's pillow, and for the first time, I talked to Crystal…her spirit.

Come on, Crystal. Make sure all goes well. Be with your little girl and give her courage, and give me the split-second reactions I need to make this go down the right way.

I tossed and turned. I was amazed at how quickly I went from love to pure hatred for Rob. The thought of him made me want to punch something. In the middle of the night, knowing sleep was hopeless, I donned a pair of shorts and a sports bra and went out to the barn. I wanted to go punch a heavy bag, punch away my hatred until it was all out of me.

When I got to the barn, it was already lit. I walked in expecting Big Jimmy, but it was Sovo, already punching one of the heavy bags.

I laughed. "You had the same idea, huh?"

The fury on his face was unmistakable. "I kill them."

I went to another punching bag and started in on it, putting all my power into the shots. My shoulder still gave me pain, but I punched through it. I kept using visualization to picture Rob's face right in front of me as I punched over and over and over again. Soon, I lost awareness of Sovo being there, of anything but my breath and the steady rhythm of my punches. Finally, I felt as if my anger was gone, and I stopped. Sovo was staring at me.

"Feel better?" he asked, cocking an eyebrow, his eyes twinkling a little.

"Yes. Not all better. I can't be all better until she's home. But I feel better, yeah."

He was over to me in three strides, tilting my head back and kissing me. We were both drenched in sweat and chest against chest. I kissed him back. The attraction had been there, forbidden, but now I wanted him. I moved from his mouth to his neck and heard him moan. Finally, I pulled away.

"Sovo…I've got to go take a cold shower. This is not the right thing for right now."

I didn't wait to see his reaction, but turned and ran out of the barn, back to the house. In my shower, I washed away the sweat and the anger, the salty confusion of my kiss with Sovo, and in its place was a sleepy exhaustion.

I crawled back into bed. I thought of Destiny, and then of being on the run with her. Pictures ran through my mind of Sovo playing Old Maid. Of all of us laughing. Of the way it felt when he had his arms around me as I practiced shooting. I fell into a deep sleep, my last thoughts of a man with a haunted past.

Big Jimmy got everyone guns and night-vision goggles. I had no idea who his supplier was, but this was costing us a fortune. Deacon was making withdrawal after withdrawal of cash from the bank.

We planned to practice with the guns around midday. First we all hiked into the canyon. I took a pad and pencil and mapped major landmarks and cacti, trying to get it accurate enough to use as a rudimentary land map.

All totaled, we would have eight men, plus me: Sovo, Big Jimmy, Terry (who insisted on coming even though his fight was days away), Deacon and four former Hell's Angels who all had tough names like Hog and Rocky. Everyone picked his hiding spot.

We hiked back out and went to the ranch for target practice.

Sovo stood in front of us all explaining how night-vision goggles worked. We tried them out in the barn, just so we could see how everything took on a greenish hue.

Next Sovo explained how to train the red pinpoint laser sight on a target and how to squeeze smoothly.

"Most important," he said, "don't rush your shot."

We had set up targets off in the distance. Terry turned out to be the best marksman after Sovo. I was the third best. We practiced over and over and over again, round after round of ammunition.

"And remember," I said, "be aware of where Destiny is at *all* times."

After target practice we went inside. Sovo had been avoiding looking at me. I hoped he could understand that I was completely overwhelmed by the circumstances, no matter how competent I appeared.

In my bedroom, I paced and changed into my clothes for the appointed meeting. I wore a gun strapped to my ankle, and one in a shoulder holster. We had said no weapons, but I knew Perrone, regardless of what Rob said, would bring bodyguards loaded with firepower.

My palms were sweating, so I took several deep breaths. Three hours before the meeting, the guys, except for Deacon, took off for the canyon. They would park a mile from the location and then hike in the back way, and get ready in their positions.

At the appointed hour, Deacon came to get me.

"Hold my hands, Jack."

I joined hands with him, and Deacon said a prayer, "Good Lord Almighty, please keep Destiny safe and return her to our fold, much as the shepherd gathers his sheep. Please keep us all safe. Let no force be necessary. We ask this in the name of Jesus Christ. Amen."

"Amen. Deacon, do you think we can trust this meeting to go down as we planned?"

"I'm placing my trust in the Lord, because I just don't know what to expect, Jack. I know that likely, in no way can they be trusted. But we're as prepared as we can be."

For the first time, probably ever, Deacon looked a little old, a little weary, tired. The strain was showing on all of us. And we still had a fight on New Year's Eve.

We climbed into his Lexus with the original tapes and headed toward the canyon. We parked in the turnoff and hiked in. Dusk was coming, and the place was alive with crimson rays from the sun.

We walked to the direct center of the small canyon, and I hoped everyone was in position and ready to go.

Standing there, I watched the canyon entrance. Two huge SUVs arrived. I guess I assumed they would hike in, like Deacon and I, putting us on equal footing as far as our vehicles being out of our reach. But they drove the SUVs right into the canyon and came within twenty feet of us and got out. I spied five bodyguards and Rob, but I didn't see Perrone, or Destiny.

Shit. They were already playing games, and I would have to think on my feet. It was as if I had watched a fight film a hundred times, and then, when the fighter came into the ring, my opponent suddenly switched to a southpaw style.

"Hello, love," Rob said.

"Where's Destiny?"

"Hmm…well, it seems that, in the end, Tony didn't trust you not to line this canyon with big men with guns." He smiled, looking up at the rocks and landmarks where our guys were hidden. He returned his gaze to me. "So me and you are going to take a little ride."

"Rob…" Deacon intoned. "Where is the child?"

"She's at the next place we're going. Just Jack and me, and these gentlemen here. Since you brought the tapes, hand them over."

The tapes were in a bag behind me. "Not a chance."

"Come on. You do it Tony's way or not at all."

"And all I have to do is send the tapes to the real FBI and Perrone does a nice stretch of time, Rob. So this isn't going to fly."

"Look, we just need a little assurance that you haven't made more copies."

"And as I told you, I want this nightmare over." Calling his bluff, I said to Deacon, "Let's go until they play fair."

Deacon nodded, and as we went to pick up the tapes, we heard the sound of several weapons having their clips inserted.

We turned back around. "So you'd kill Jack?" Deacon asked. "For money? For what? Rob, you were part of this family. How could you go so wrong, son?"

"Don't 'son' me. I wanted to marry her, Deacon, but her old man—and you—and every goddamn fighter in this camp always came before me."

"But that's not true. She loved you. Now, fair is fair, Rob, we had a deal about how this was going to go down."

"No. Jack thought, like always, that she was going to call all the shots. But this time, I'm in charge, and we do it my way."

"And where do you plan on taking me, Rob?"

"To Destiny. I promise you. I'm taking you to her. We swap the tapes, you answer a few questions, and I literally let you walk out the door, into a cab, and you can go live your life. Tony will have what he wants."

"Let me come, too," Deacon said, "and you have a deal."

Rob put his hands up. "Oh, no. This is between Jack and me."

I didn't see as I had a choice. I had to get Destiny back. "Fine. Let my uncle go. Let him walk out of the canyon."

"No. We do it this way." Suddenly Rob pulled a gun out and pointed it at me.

"Hand me your gun, Jack. Don't you know nice girls shouldn't play with guns?"

I moved to get my gun from my shoulder holster, and he said, "Slowly. You wouldn't want one of these guys to think you were making a move on me."

Slowly, I did as I was told and threw the gun on the ground between us.

Rob aimed his gun at Deacon next. "Now you."

Deacon reluctantly took his gun from his waistband holster and also tossed it on the ground.

"Now, Jack, pick up the tapes."

I bent over and picked them up and moved toward Rob, who grabbed me roughly by the arm and started to direct me toward one of the SUVs. At that moment, two shots rang out and two bodyguards went down. One was shot in the shoulder, and the other grabbed his leg. I knew it was Sovo. And maybe Terry, our newly discovered marksman.

Rob grabbed me by my hair and dragged me to the SUV, opening the door and shoving me inside. Deacon had hit the ground to take cover and was facedown in the dust. Another bodyguard was picked off by our guys in the canyon, and the remaining two got into the SUV.

The doors slammed and locked, and Rob pressed a gun to my neck.

"What about the guys?" the driver asked, gesturing toward the men lying on the canyon floor wounded.

"Leave 'em. Let's rock 'n' roll."

Through tinted windows, I looked back helplessly and saw my guys coming out of their hiding spots and racing to Deacon's side. With a sinking feeling, I wondered if I would ever see them all again.

Chapter 21

"You lied to me, Jack."

Rob had let go of my hair, but he still had a gun trained on me. My scalp tingled with pain.

"Jesus Christ, Rob," I snarled. "If you want to get into a pissing contest about who's done the most lying, you'd win hands down, you fucking bastard."

He leaned over and started kissing me, forcing his tongue into my mouth. I resisted, and he pulled back, glaring at me.

"No kiss? What? Saving that for Sovo?"

I rolled my eyes, and he grabbed me roughly again, forcing himself on me, probing into my mouth with his tongue. I bit it, drawing blood.

"Fuck…fuck! God, you fucking bitch," he snapped, and hit me with a backhand.

I folded my arms and stared out the window.

"We were good together, Jack. If it wasn't for your friend Crystal, butting her nose in where it didn't belong, we would be on our way to a nice life."

I didn't answer. The slap had stung, but I resisted the urge to rub my face. I didn't want him to see me nervous, or see that he had hurt me.

We drove on through the night into the heart of Vegas. I watched my surroundings, trying to figure out where we were going. I soon realized we were going back to the same disgusting warehouse where I had met the so-called FBI agent. The glimmer of hope, in my mind, was that Sovo might remember the address and think of the warehouse and try to find me. The other little glimmer was the fact that Rob had taken the gun from my shoulder holster but not the small gun attached to my calf.

We arrived at the warehouse, and Rob roughly pulled me out of the SUV. We walked inside, and Tony Perrone was waiting with Destiny, who was coloring and had what looked like a new and very expensive porcelain doll with Shirley Temple curls and a hoop skirt.

"Auntie Jack!" she squealed, and came running toward me. Perrone, dressed in an expensive suit, probably custom-made, gave the slightest of nods, and his guys, including Rob, backed away from me and allowed us a little reunion. I knelt down and brushed back the hair from her face and kissed her on the cheek.

"Hey, it sure is good to see you," I said, trying not to let my voice shake and reveal what a mess I had found myself in. I wanted her to feel secure that we would both be going home very soon.

"I missed you," she said, nuzzling against my neck.

"I missed you, too. And so has Big Jimmy and Uncle Deacon and Sovo and Eddie."

"Can we go home now?"

"Well, it seems like your uncle Tony has a few things he wants to go over with me."

"Destiny," Tony said a little sternly. "Come here and sit at the table, while I talk to your *auntie* Jack." He said the word "auntie" with sarcasm and his lips were curled into a sneer.

She did as she was told, and Perrone signaled to Rob to sit with her. Because she knew him, I suppose they hoped that would keep her calm.

Taking me over to the side, Perrone said, "Where are the tapes?"

"That guy there has them." I pointed to a bodyguard with the duffel bag.

"And where are my other men?"

"Well, being as you didn't play fair, my guess is they're in an ambulance somewhere."

"I keep having to give hazard pay to the men I've hired to hunt you down."

"You could have just asked nicely."

He smiled menacingly. "I heard you had a smart mouth."

"Don't believe everything you hear."

He leaned in very close to me. "I want to get out of this piss-and-oil cesspool as quickly as you do, but we have a small little problem."

"What's that?"

"How can I trust a woman who set my house on fire, has shot my men, who set up an ambush in the canyon where I sent my men to meet her…who, in short, is a giant pain in the ass to me?"

"First of all, all of that happened because *you* started it. The men were in the canyon because we guessed you would arrive with firepower, and you did. You're the one fucking with us."

"Well, we still need to find out if you're telling the truth. Now, I don't want to upset little Destiny. She's like my own child. So we're going to take you to the other end of the warehouse. We have a—how shall I put this?—a temporary boxing ring set up. And we'll find out if you're telling the truth, once and for all. Then we can be done with each other and move on." He wiped his hands together to symbolize being finished.

I swallowed hard. I prayed that Deacon and Sovo and the rest of them were figuring out where I was. I didn't believe in telepathy, but in my mind, I spoke to Sovo. *Come find me. Come find me. Come find me.*

"Destiny?" Tony said.

"Yes, Uncle Tony?"

"I need to go speak with your *delightful* auntie Jack in private. Rob will keep you company until we come back, okay?"

I smiled at Destiny, trying not to let her see how dire our situation was. Rob gave me a leering look as I left with Perrone and one of his bodyguards, a guy easily the size of Big Jimmy. Maybe bigger.

They led me to an area at the far end of the warehouse. They had cleared out a square area, about the size of a boxing ring, and it was illuminated by an industrial light hanging from the metal rafters. Wooden boxes marked the four corners like the posts in a real ring.

"Ever fight bare-knuckles style, Jack?" Perrone asked me. "Without the gloves. Like real men."

"Real men don't beat up women and kidnap innocent children."

"That mouth again. Tommy, hold her."

The big bodyguard pinned my arms tightly behind my back. Perrone came close to me with a roll of duct tape. I shook my head from side to side. "Shh," he said. "I don't like that fresh mouth of yours. In fact, I've been telling Rob for some time that he should find himself a beautiful showgirl to fuck him all night long and forget about this tough brunette who was always making him crazy, anyway."

I spat in his face.

"Tsk, tsk. See, that's what this duct tape is for. I'm going to tape your mouth closed, so that when Tommy beats the *living shit* out of you, little Destiny doesn't have to hear it. And I don't have to listen to your smart mouth."

Roughly, he grabbed my face in one hand and tore off a big piece of duct tape with his teeth. Then he slammed it over my mouth tightly as I glared at him.

"Oh, I see the hatred in your eyes. It doesn't bother me. You see, you can't get to be a man of my wealth and my position without someone hating you, all the little people that you step on along the way."

Tommy let go of my arms and pushed me into the ring. It wasn't canvas beneath my feet, but concrete. It was going to hurt like hell every time I hit it, so I needed to stay on my feet.

Tommy took off his suit jacket and rolled up his shirtsleeves. He was easily six foot one, with the build of a football linebacker. His arms were the size of my *thighs*.

Perrone sneered. "I'm going to ask you a series of yes or no questions. You don't need your mouth for that. Just nod for yes or shake your head for no. I'll ask every time you hit the ground, and we'll pull you up until you can't stand any longer, and then we'll call that a technical knockout of our own. Okay?"

I inhaled through my nose and sized up my opponent. I needed to think like a boxer and think like a sniper. What did I notice about this guy Tommy? I fought the panic. *Stay calm, Jack. You can do this.* He was a rightie. Not a southpaw. He smelled of smoke, meaning he might wind easily, as smokers often do.

I couldn't show fear. Find the angry spot, I told myself. I was plenty pissed, so that wasn't too hard.

Perrone said, "I don't have a bell…but you can begin."

Tommy and I circled each other, and Perrone stood just on the outside of the mock ring.

Tommy came closer to me and swung. I ducked and slugged him in the stomach then moved back quickly out of the range of his arms.

"Now, Tommy," Perrone chided. "You're not going to let yourself get beaten by a girl, are you?"

Tommy charged at me more angrily, looking like a bull charging a matador. He landed a punch in my ribs. I heard a cracking sound and fell like a ton of bricks. I couldn't get air through my mouth, so it was doubly hard to recover.

Perrone shouted his question from outside the ring. "Are there any copies of the tapes?"

I shook my head, trying to keep calm. My eyes were tearing involuntarily from the pain, which was searing.

"Help her up, Tommy. Be a gentleman."

I waved off Tommy's help. I stood as pain scorched through my side. I shifted my weight from side to side, moved my head from side to side, trying to clear my mind. Tommy circled me again, but I danced always out of his reach. I decided there wasn't much sense in trying to hit him. I wouldn't be able to bring him down except with a lucky shot. And he stood at least eight inches taller, plus those tree-trunk arms and legs of his. But I could avoid getting hit as long as possible. Maybe by then I would be found.

Tommy came at me again. In the course of defending myself, I landed a punch at his nose and drew blood, then retreated out of reach again.

"Pussy," Perrone sneered. "Do I have to get Carlos to take this fight?"

Tommy shook his head and came at me, landing a blow to my jaw. Even though it just grazed my jaw, it was powerful, like being hit with an iron crowbar. I fell to the ground and felt blood in my mouth where I had bit my cheek because I wasn't wearing a mouth guard.

"Again, Jack, are there any more copies of the tape?"

I shook my head and climbed up again. Hatred coursed through my veins and settled like a fire in my belly.

He hit me again in the ribs, and I felt bile rising in me, though I didn't topple over.

Then Tommy threw another shot to the side of my face; this one landed with rock-hard precision. When I fell, I hit my head hard on the concrete floor and saw stars.

"Try to avoid the face, Tommy. It'll frighten the child. With any luck, a few shots and she'll have some internal bleeding and that may be the end of her."

I lay there, looking up and seeing the world in a haze. Then I recalled the beating my father took when I was little. I asked him if he was afraid to go into the ring again, and he said, "No. Because it's not always the stronger man who wins, but the smarter man."

I would have to be smarter. I would have to turn my body when the blows came and lower myself a little so I took them in the arm, if possible. I also knew I couldn't take too much more. *Stay smart, Jack,* I told myself.

I got up slowly and circled Tommy, trying to be the smarter fighter. I "used the ring," which was fight talk for moving all over the ring and trying to put distance between you and the other fighter while wearing him out. I couldn't match Tommy for raw power, but I could surpass him in endurance.

I noticed he was winded. He wasn't moving as fast. I avoided his blows, but again he caught me in the face and I hit the ground, landing on my shoulder, so I faced away from Perrone and Tommy. I didn't move.

"Did you knock her out?" Perrone asked.

"Think so, boss."

"Get her up."

But I didn't want Tommy coming near me. If I didn't do something soon, I would be dead inside of ten minutes. I had nothing to lose.

I was swallowing quantities of blood. Moving my hands, I removed, painfully, the duct tape and puked all over the floor, dark red and smelling of blood.

"Remember, don't scream, Jack. You'll frighten the baby."

I said nothing, but, my back to them, I spit blood on the floor.

"Have you told anyone else about these tapes? The FBI? Anyone?"

"No. I just want my life back, Perrone."

"Should I believe her, Tommy? I think she needs a few more body shots. I'd like to see her lose a spleen or something. If you get her liver, she's a goner. The liver is right here." My back was to him, but I assumed he was pointing to the precise location he wanted Tommy to hit.

To distract them, I leaned forward and stuck my finger down my throat and threw up again. As I did so, I raised my pant leg and grabbed my gun—whirling around and shooting Perrone in the shoulder in one swift shot. He went down and I pointed the gun at Tommy, who raised his hands as the other bodyguard came running. I could hear Destiny's shriek.

Perrone started to make a groaning noise, and I shot him in the leg, at which he screamed. I saw blood forming around him on the floor, dark red fanning out like an amoeba.

I could barely see out of my eye because my cheek had swelled so much. Keeping the gun on both bodyguards, moving it from one to the other, I made my way backward to where Rob and Destiny were.

Destiny started crying the minute she saw my face.

"It's okay, sweetie, Auntie Jack is okay. We're going to go home now."

The two bodyguards had helped Perrone to his feet. He was shrieking, "Get me to a fucking doctor!"

"Destiny," I said as best I could through swollen lips, "come here."

But Rob grabbed her and pulled out his own gun. She came up to his waist, and he held her to him by pulling on her braid. She was screaming.

"Shut up!" he yelled at her. She held her hand to her mouth, but she grew quiet. I saw her trembling.

"It's okay, baby," I soothed her. "It's okay. Rob, you know you're not going to do this, so let her go. You have the tapes. You have what you wanted from the start."

"Not a chance. You come with us, and we release the girl to Deacon."

"Your time for bargaining is over."

I trained the gun on his chest. Suddenly, I heard a commotion behind me as Sovo, Deacon and the guys ran into the warehouse calling my and Destiny's names.

"Over here!" I yelled.

They found us and were moving closer to us when Rob said, "One more step and the kid buys it."

"Rob," I said firmly, "it's over. Let her go and get a head start on the cops."

"No. This isn't going down the way you want, Jack. You are not running the show here. Why couldn't you have just let things go? Huh? Why'd you have to question?"

I trained the red pinpoint laser sight right on his chest. He looked down and saw he was a marked man.

"I'll kill her, I swear it, Jack."

From behind me, I heard the calm words of Sovo as he said, "Take the shot."

I did.

Chapter 22

Rob fell, the gun clattering across the floor. Destiny ran to me and buried her head into my belly.

I collapsed to the floor as sirens screeched. Sovo and Big Jimmy held Perrone and his bodyguards at gunpoint as officers raced into the building. Someone checked the pulse at Rob's carotid artery.

"This one...he's dead," the officer said. He opened Rob's shirt and saw he was shot right in the heart.

I had killed the man I once trusted. Sovo and Deacon stood over me. "Stay with us, Jack," Deacon urged. He knelt down. "Focus on my face." Then he laid hands on me. "Bring her healing, Lord."

And then...blackness.

* * *

I woke up to the sound of unfamiliar beeping and pain—more pain than I had ever experienced in my whole life. The closest I ever came was the time my appendix almost burst. My eyelids fluttered, and I was aware that my cheek was swollen so much that it had shut my eye. I tried to see through one eye. I wanted to know where I was.

A nurse was standing over me.

"I'm Claire," she said. "You're in the hospital, Jackie. You're safe. I'm the private-duty nurse your uncle hired. Do you need some pain medication?"

Did I need pain medication? I needed morphine. Fast. I tried to nod my head, but found any movement hurt, so I just gave her a pleading look and blinked my eyes three times. Y-e-s.

Five minutes later, someone was putting morphine into my IV line and I felt as if I were floating, and then, sweet blackness.

I don't know when I woke next. Claire was there again. She had blond hair and a crisp white uniform—old-fashioned looking. She was about forty-five, and she smelled of baby powder. She smiled at me.

"You're going to be okay, you know."

I blinked three times, which now seemed to be my code for yes.

"I'm going to go get your uncle and your friend, Sovo."

I grabbed her hand and mouthed the words "little girl."

"Oh, that sweet child is fine. As fine as she can be considering all she's been through. Look." Claire held up a picture Destiny had colored with flowers and a rainbow on it. "She made you this get-well card."

I tried to smile and found it only worked on one side. The other was too swollen.

Claire left the room, then Deacon and Sovo came in. Sovo looked as if he was at a funeral. His face was pale, and he had deep circles under his eyes and a haggard look. He was unshaven. Deacon didn't look too much better.

Deacon took my hand. "Jack, your father knows everything that's gone on. We already have an attorney working on his release, and we even have a judge and the prosecutor's office talking to each other. Those tapes will free him and bring down a Vegas empire."

I shut my eyes gratefully.

"Rob is dead, you know."

I tried to nod.

"I didn't know what you remembered. You've got four broken ribs, and some minor internal bleeding, a concussion and a hairline fracture on your skull from when you must have hit the concrete. The swelling will eventually go down. Your cheekbone is shattered, and we'll see how it heals. They're bringing in a plastic surgeon on a consult. You'll be out in two or three days, we hope."

I tried my voice, a cross between a whisper and a rasp. "Everyone else?"

"Fine. We're all fine. The fight is still on. You just may be home for it. You can watch it on pay-per-view."

"No. I'm going."

"Good Lord, but you're crazy. Let's make sure you're even well enough to go home." He leaned down to kiss me. "I don't ever want to be scared like that again. And you should know, the police chief is on administrative leave. This whole thing is taking quite a bit of unraveling. At first, I thought we might be looking at some weapons charges against us, but there are so many bigger fish to fry, and being as a corrupt police department was one of the issues, they seem to have backed off that idea."

Deacon stood straight again and clapped Sovo on the back. "See, I told you, Sovo. Faith."

He looked from Sovo to me and back again. "I think I'll give you two a few moments alone."

He left, and Sovo knelt by my bedside and put his lips to my hand, avoiding the IV needle. "I thought I would die seeing you like this."

"I must be a sight."

"Just you opening your eyes is the most beautiful sight I've ever seen."

"Thanks." It hurt to talk because my throat was so dry.

"In my country, I killed as a soldier. It's not…personal. In the warehouse, I wanted to make it very personal."

He stood and wiped some hair from my brow, kissing my forehead. "I'm glad you're going to be okay."

I mouthed the words, "Me, too."

Chapter 23

It was amazing what twenty-four hours could do.

My doctor stood at the foot of my bed, looking at his clipboard. He was a young guy, midthirties, with a shaved head that gave him a "Hollywood cool" look instead of, from what I could see, a receding hairline. "As I told you, Jackie, there's not much we can do about the broken ribs or the hairline skull fracture. You'll have to come back for another CAT scan of the head in a week. As for the ribs, we can put a supportive bandage there, but ultimately, they just have to heal, so you're going to be sore for a while.

"Once you're released, you'll follow up on your

plastic surgery consult. The bruising and swelling will subside over time. Your blood counts all look excellent, so your internal bleeding is okay. No anemia. Your white blood count looks good, so no hidden infections. We'll send you home with some painkillers, and you'll need to let us know if they're working for you. Now, once you're released, I'd like you to check in with my nurse once a day, just to monitor some of the symptoms of breathlessness, as well as your pain level."

I nodded.

"The swelling in your knuckles should subside." He picked up my hand. "Personally, I'm glad you gave that son of a bitch a few punches."

I gave a half smile, the only kind I could for right now.

"And, I want you to take it easy. Okay?"

"I don't think anyone will let me do otherwise."

"Good…" He paused.

"What is it, Dr. Fielding?"

"I just want to say that you are gutsier than any patient I've ever had. What you did to rescue that little girl… And I have to say, if it wasn't for your superb physical condition, you would be looking at far more serious problems right now. I don't know—" he swallowed hard "—what kind of a monster does this to a woman. I've seen it in rape cases, women beaten, domestic violence. I will never understand the evil of some men. I admire your courage."

"Thanks."

After the doctor left, two FBI agents came in. They'd taken statements from everyone.

"Joe Gallagher," the first one, a very tall man with short black hair, said.

"Tim Snelling," the second one chimed in. He had brown hair and wore sunglasses, which he took off as he introduced himself.

They both held out their hands, but I said, "Sorry, guys. I fractured my knuckles trying to hit that giant, and I can't do a handshake."

"Our apologies."

"None needed."

"We think we have everything," Agent Gallagher said. "Perrone, apparently, wanted to increase his control over pay-per-view and over fighters that he was bankrolling. And he and Bonita saw a way to consolidate the power. Plus Bonita had assembled a gambling consortium." The agent shook his head. "Doesn't seem like there's ever enough money for these guys."

"And Rob?" I refused to cry over him, but I had never killed a man before, and I certainly didn't want to ever have to again.

"Interesting. We went sifting through his apartment. Seems he was in deep to the casinos. Debt to Tony Perrone, who was only too happy to exchange your boyfriend being a spy in your camp for erasure of the debt. Perrone is now trying to say he had no idea of Rob's plan and he's passing it all off, but of course your injuries with him standing right there attest to the opposite. Everyone's finger-pointing, of course, and Chief Dillard is actually saying he was trying to get evidence against Perrone, though no official case file or report exists."

"These guys sure can spin a web of lies."

"Yeah. Some real tall tales."

"Perrone's injuries?"

"The leg was more serious. He's fine, though. Cops are posted outside his hospital room." Then he added, "Different hospital."

"Thank God for that. I don't ever want to see him again unless he's in shackles."

"Well, he's already lawyered up. And not just any attorney. He's got the asshole Jason White. Guy charges a thousand an hour or something crazy like that, but Perrone has more money than God, so it's no big deal."

"Please tell me he won't get off."

"Not likely. Not likely at all. But trust me, his attorney will try to suppress evidence and do everything possible, every dirty trick, to make it go his way."

"I wish I…I don't know…Rob had us all so muddled, and then I met that fake FBI agent, and so I wish I had gone to the real feds."

"That fake FBI agent was actually another cop on the take."

"This runs all through Vegas, doesn't it?"

"Sure does."

"But if I had found you guys, maybe none of this would have happened."

"Look," the taller FBI agent said. "You don't know that. You did what you thought was right at the time. All you wanted was to keep that child safe."

"It all just went so crazy. I'm sorry."

"No. If you hadn't been set up with a fake FBI agent, you might have felt you could have trusted the guys with the badges. Anyway, we won't keep you right now. We'll be in touch."

"And my dad?"

"Things look good, though, it won't move as fast as you'd like. We'll move it along as quickly as we can."

The agents left, and Big Jimmy and Sovo arrived with armloads of flowers.

"I've never been a big flower kind of girl, guys," I teased. "But they're beautiful."

They put them down on the windowsill. Big Jimmy came over to me. "I would have gone crazy if she was hurt, Jack."

"So would I."

"I owe you her life, my life. I—"

"Jimmy, none of us would have let anything happen to her."

Sovo leaned down to give me a kiss. "From now on, I'm the only one getting beat up, okay?" he joked.

I clicked on the television with my remote control. "There's supposed to be a press conference in a little while."

Sovo sat gently on my bed and Big Jimmy sat in

the armchair next to us. We watched our local news channel. An attorney, whose name was flashed as Jason White, stood in back of a podium. He wore an expensive suit with diamond cuff links that glittered in the sunlight on the steps where he was giving his press conference.

"At two o'clock this afternoon, my client, Mr. Tony Perrone, who has been a model citizen, a fixture of philanthropic events here in Las Vegas, and is a businessman who generates jobs and money in the community, was granted bail in the sum of five million dollars. Though we find that sum outrageous, considering that he is most certainly not a flight risk, he posted bail immediately and was ushered out from the basement of the police department and is at this time in his home again, where he belongs."

"Oh, my God!" I yelled at the TV. If I could have, I would have taken the set and thrown it out the window.

"What is particularly egregious about the events here is that Mr. Perrone, as many of you know, lost his fiancée just weeks ago." He paused for effect. "He is a grieving man, who has also lost the company of the child he helped raise. His fiancée was truly the light of his life."

"I can't believe this guy," Big Jimmy said.

White paused again. "And now scurrilous charges are being bandied about, something I will not stand for. I am warning the media, law enforcement and anyone associated with this case that if there is so much as a hint of slander or untruth in any statements, we will come down like the wrath of God."

"What a fucking creep," I said. "It's a wonder he can stand up. Slime like that should just ooze along the ground."

"In the meantime, we will be holding press conferences from time to time to update the media and defend Mr. Perrone's flawless and spotless reputation from the kind of character assassination that is taking place. Thank you."

As bulbs flashed and media types shouted questions, he said, "No further comment," and was ushered away by bodyguards of the big and ugly type favored by Tony Perrone.

"I think I'm going to be sick." I took the remote and clicked off the television. My blood pressure probably shot up twenty points.

"Desperate moves by desperate men," said Big Jimmy.

"What about Bonita?" I asked. I seemed to have lost an entire twenty-four hour period in a haze of drugs and pain.

Big Jimmy answered, "They're still deciding on charges. He's probably going to turn himself in tomorrow. He'll post bail and be at the fight tomorrow night."

"Won't the boxing commission ban him?"

Sovo answered, "He can't be in the ring, but he can be in the audience."

"God, what is it going to take to get these guys into jail on a more permanent basis?"

"Trial and conviction," Big Jimmy said. "Trial and conviction."

Chapter 24

New Year's Eve. I was released early in the day, though I still moved very stiffly. Sovo came alone to take me home as Deacon, Big Jimmy and Terry were preparing for the big fight against Jake Johnson.

"You look better," Sovo said.

When they took out my IVs, Claire had helped me take a shower. Because of my broken ribs, swollen knuckles and other various injuries, I couldn't raise my arms above my head. She shampooed my hair very, very gently, and helped me dress in street clothes.

"*Better* being a relative term." I pulled down the visor of Deacon's car and surveyed myself in the mirror. My face hadn't yet returned to anything close to normal. "Destiny is going to be scared of me."

"No. We told her you look hurt but are doing good. She knows you saved her life, Jack."

I swallowed hard. How had I, Jack Rooney, become this kid-loving softie? Though I was still tough enough to hold my own against the bad guys. I mustn't forget that.

"I think you look beautiful."

"You sustain a head injury, too?"

"When you knew I would die for you, to protect you, on the road, how did that make you feel about me?"

"Honestly?"

He nodded.

"Honestly, I would find myself looking at you and wondering what it would be like to kiss you. I knew you were a different kind of man."

"Which is why you are beautiful. You were willing to exchange your life for Destiny's. You are more beautiful to me now than the first time I saw you."

I lowered my head and grinned softly.

"Do you remember the first time we met?" he asked.

"I remember you coming to the gym in the city. Deacon and you hitting it off. I remember thinking you were different. You never wasted a punch. I didn't know it was because you were trained to be careful, to be sure of your shot."

"I remember you were wearing gray sweatpants

and a black tank top, and your hair was loose around your face. And I remember thinking that I would do anything to be near you."

I reached over a swollen hand to pat his leg. "I wish we hadn't lost so much time, you know, not being together."

"This way, we're close already. We skip over... what you say...the bullshit."

"Thank you, Sovo. For everything."

We drove in companionable silence. I was still, partially, coming to grips with the events of the last few weeks. My life had been turned upside down and backward. Five weeks ago, Rob had been alive and we had discussed marriage, and now he was dead. Deacon said the FBI agents told him Rob's mother, who I had met a few times and who seemed like a lovely woman, had come to claim the body. She was in a state of shock that he had been involved in a little girl's kidnapping, let alone that I had shot him while he threatened to kill Destiny. How would she explain *those* circumstances to her bridge club? I wondered.

"Sovo...it's like, in my heart, I never loved Rob." He nodded, and we rode onto the ranch property. Unmarked federal cars stood on the perimeter. Sure, *now* we've got protection. Nonetheless, it was better late than never.

Sovo parked the car and climbed out, then came over to my side and opened the door, helping me out. Deacon said he had hired Claire to come help me once a day for about two hours—showering and dressing. I ached in every muscle and every bone. Even my damn eyelashes hurt.

Slowly, leaning on Sovo, I walked into the ranch house. No place, not the most expensive hotel or mansion I have ever been in, ever looked as good.

"She's home!" I heard Destiny squeal, and she ran to me.

"No hugging," Deacon warned her gently. "Remember how I said we have to be extra careful around her."

I tousled Destiny's hair. "Don't worry, kiddo, in a few days I'll be as good as new."

She looked up into my face. "Does it hurt much?"

I gave a little nod. "Yeah. It hurts. But I'll be okay."

Deacon gave me a peck on the cheek. "Terry's out in the barn," he said. "He's worked up about tonight. Nerves."

"Tell him not to let the last few weeks influence him. If he just follows our game plan, he'll be all right."

"You're not planning on going tonight, are you?"

"Nothing could keep me away."

"Dang you, girl."

"Deacon, this is the culmination of our dream."

The phone rang, and Eddie went to answer it. Deacon said, "Media's been calling at all hours wanting quotes about Bonita, Perrone, the fight. It's been a madhouse."

"Jack," Eddie said, coming back into the den. "Your father is on the phone."

I walked into the kitchen and picked up the portable phone. "Hello?"

"Hello, tiger."

"Good to hear your voice, Dad."

"Even better to hear yours. I won't relax until I hug you for myself. Check you from head to toe and make sure you're okay. My God, but you gave me a fright. Deacon, too. He said he aged ten years in three days."

"I hear you may be coming home soon."

"Looks that way. Considering they now have *much* bigger fish to fry, the D.A. appears willing to recommend immediate release."

"That's great, Dad."

"You were awfully brave, kiddo," he said. I smiled. That was what I called Destiny. Somehow, my life was coming full circle.

"Thanks."

"And I hear, from a little bird, that Sovo and you…" He trailed off.

"Rumors are true," I said, grinning.

"I always liked that boy. He's going to be the next Terry Keenan, you know."

"I know."

"Well, listen, until I get out of here, I'm just a number, and there are guys waiting for the phone." As always I could hear the noises of the prison behind him. Lots of shouts and trash talking.

"Bye, Dad. I love you."

"Love you, too."

I hung up, and Deacon said, "All right, here are the plans. Big Jimmy's mother is coming to watch Destiny."

I looked down at Destiny. She grinned. "I have a new grandma."

"Cool, kiddo."

"Eddie, me, Terry and Jimmy are going to the Majestic in the van and get settled into our locker room, get comfortable."

"Okay."

"You and Sovo follow whenever you're ready. You've got ringside seats. Get there early, because I don't want you jostled in the crowd."

"Okay."

"And if you don't feel well, stay home and watch it on pay-per-view."

"Deacon, Tony Perrone owns the Majestic. Won't the press be going crazy over us and him being there at the same time?"

"We handle things with grace and dignity, Jack. 'Cause he's just living on borrowed time and it won't be too long before he trades in that palace of his for a jail cell like your daddy's."

"You'll steer clear of him, won't you?"

"Sure, we will. But the Majestic already hired extra security because of the media."

"Yeah. Extra security that reports to *him*."

"We'll have our own guys there. It'll go down just

fine, Jack. Don't you worry. And if it makes you uneasy, stay home. No shame in staying home."

I thrust my chin forward. "He's not going to scare me away from being there when Terry wins."

Chapter 25

Big Jimmy's mother, whom we all called Mama Bear, arrived and immediately took Destiny into the kitchen to cook something deliciously sweet and decadent. Destiny told me Big Jimmy had introduced Mama Bear to her while I was in the hospital. Mama Bear cried and said Destiny looked just like Jimmy. She was a proud grandma, with a long, gray braid that she wrapped around in a bun, and weathered honey-colored skin. She kissed me before taking Destiny into the kitchen. "Good girl," she said.

Sovo came with me into my bedroom. Destiny's things had now been shifted to her own room right next door to Big Jimmy's. He would lie on the floor next to her bed in a sleeping bag until she fell asleep, and then leave his door open all night in case she got scared and wanted to come into his room.

In my bedroom, I slumped onto the bed.

"Tired?" Sovo's face registered concern.

I nodded. "I hurt more than I let on."

"You don't have to pretend for me."

"I know. That's why I just told you." I smiled. I would have winked, but my swollen face prevented that.

"Want to take a bath? It would help sore muscles."

"You know, that sounds really good, Sovo." In the hospital, Claire had helped me in the shower by sitting me on a chair while she scrubbed my hair and caked dried blood off of me.

"Wait here." He went into my bathroom and began drawing water. My tub is a big Roman one with Jacuzzi jets, though I didn't think my ribs could handle being jostled by the jets. Still, a long soak would feel heavenly.

Coming back into my room, Sovo walked to me and unbuttoned my shirt. Immediately, I felt shivers at his touch. I stood, and he helped me off with my top, then my bra, leaning down to kiss each breast.

"This is no fair if I get naked and you don't," I said with a grin.

He pulled his shirt over his head. Then he knelt and slowly took my sweatpants off, kissing his way down my belly. It was hard to breathe.

I slipped my shoes off as he pulled my sweats

completely off, then he took off his jeans. We stood, naked, facing each other, and just pressed our chests against each other. Leading me by the hand, he took me to the steaming tub. He climbed in, then I climbed in and leaned my back against his chest.

He turned off the water, and the two of us just soaked in silence. He had lit a candle and it created warm shadows on the wall, flickering. Periodically, he would take the bar of soap and wash my breasts and belly, gently enough to drive me wild.

"Sorry to disappoint you, Sovo, but until I heal, no hot sex action."

He laughed out loud, and I realized I didn't often hear him laugh. I hoped to change that in the future. I wanted to hear him laugh often and loudly.

"What's so funny?"

"You. This is good enough for me right now. I just want to hold you."

I turned my head to the side and lay my cheek against his chest. I was so warm and comfortable, I almost dozed off.

When the water cooled, he helped me stand, then wrapped me gently in two towels. He dried me off and helped me back to the bedroom, so I could pick clothes to wear to the fight. Ordinarily, I dress in black velvet pants and a dressy shirt or jacket. Ringside seats mean sitting with "the beautiful people"— though with my face, I didn't feel that description *quite* fit me.

I stood at my closet. "I can wear these velvet pants because they're elastic-waisted. I can't wear anything I have to work too hard at to get on and off. What if I have to use the bathroom? And..." I looked through my tops. "This one buttons easily but still looks nice. I'll wear it with a camisole underneath it. Nothing too tight on my ribs. No heels. I'll wear these flats."

Sovo helped me dress. When he finished, I stood on tiptoe and kissed him on the lips, biting his bottom lip gently. He sighed. "You do that...I can't get dressed." He looked down at his growing erection.

"Sorry!" I laughed. He wrapped a towel around his waist and walked to his room, where he dressed in black pants, a black silk T-shirt and a black leather jacket.

He came back with two guns. One for me, and one for him.

"I thought I was through with all this shit."

"If Perrone and Bonita are there, I carry."

"What if you get stopped by Security?"

He opened his wallet. He had a carry-and-conceal permit.

I looked down at my hands. "I'm not positive I could even squeeze the trigger if I had to."

Sovo took the clip out of one of the guns and put the gun in my right hand. I was surprised that I could still pull the trigger smoothly. "Okay. I would feel better if I had it. But when Perrone and Bonita are locked up, I don't care if I ever see another gun as long as I live. In fact, I would prefer not to!"

We left my bedroom and went to say goodbye to Mama Bear and Destiny.

"You look beautiful," Destiny gushed.

"Thanks. You having fun?"

She nodded. "Mama Bear said I look just like my daddy when he was little." She ran over to the kitchen table and brought back a picture clearly taken in the early 1960s, judging by the clothes. "This is my dad," she pointed. "And this is Mama Bear."

Mama Bear gazed at the camera, her long black hair to her waist. "You were quite a looker, Mama," I said.

"Wasn't she beautiful?" Destiny asked.

Sovo patted her head. "You are beautiful, too."

"Did you know, Auntie Jack, that I asked Big Jimmy if I could call him Daddy and he said yes?"

"That's great, kiddo."

"Have a good time tonight."

"We will," I said.

We left the ranch and drove toward Las Vegas. Soon, we hit the glitz and glamour of the Strip, a place where neon rose high in the sky and made the city glow from a distance. I've lived in Nevada all my life, raised in arenas and squalid gyms, casinos and hotels. But still, after all this time, I get a tiny thrill when I see the lights of Vegas. The action, the energy, fills me up with excitement.

Sovo reached over and touched my cheek, his

thumb just barely rubbing where the swelling was. "I kill him next time."

"There won't be a next time."

We arrived at the Majestic and left our car with the valet. The lobby was a sight to behold. The theme of the hotel was "royalty," and so it aimed for over-the-top glamour and elegance in a sort of Italian Renaissance flavor. The service was supposed to make you feel like a king or a queen. The ceiling in the main lobby was an exact replica of the Sistine Chapel. It was the most ambitious mural project ever tried in a hotel, at least that's what the Travel Channel said.

The carpets were thick and plush and you sort of sank in them as you walked. Gilded fixtures gleamed.

We walked through the casino and then toward the huge auditorium where the fight was to be held. Sovo and I both had badges hanging around our necks that identified us as belonging to Terry Keenan's official camp. We walked down a very long tunnel-like hallway to our locker room, our voices echoing in the hall. Thankfully, considering the tensions between the two camps, Jake's locker room was on the exact opposite side of the auditorium. No chance of any of us meeting before the fight began.

"Hey, gang," I said, smiling as I walked in.

"Jack!" Terry came rushing over to me and kissed the top of my head.

Eddie the Geek took off his glasses and welled up.

"Good God, Eddie, don't start that or we'll all be blubbering," I said.

Everyone laughed. I looked at Terry. "How you feeling?"

"Trying to stay loose," he said.

In the locker room, the idea was to build up a little sweat before the fight, to stay loose and to warm up the muscles.

Deacon asked us all to join hands for a prefight prayer. We formed a circle and held hands. Sovo gripped my pinkie only, in deference to my swollen hand. We bowed our heads. I raised mine slightly to look around the circle with gratitude we were all alive, all together.

"Gracious Father, heavenly Lord, we gather here already strengthened by the miracle of the bravery, courage and strength of our Jack. And now we also ask you to bless this warrior, Terry Keenan. He's a good man who has trained hard and worked to become a better man and a better fighter. Please bless our team…Eddie, Big Jimmy, Sovo… all of us. Guide us to keep you in the forefront of our lives and our heart. We ask this in the name of Jesus Christ who shed his precious blood for us, Amen."

"Amen," we all said in unison.

There was a knock on the locker room door. Deacon said, "Come in," assuming it was someone from the boxing commission or the in-house doctor. No one else, no media, had the passes necessary to come down the tunnel.

Tony Perrone strode in with a phalanx of body-guards. He was walking with a cane. Next to me, I felt Sovo stiffen and watched his eyes go cold and serious.

"Jack," Perrone mocked. "Good to see you up and about. I'm just here as the owner of the Majestic, to wish you *well*. Let's put on a good fight for the people who have shelled out lots and lots of money for an exciting show, shall we?"

Deacon's voice trembled. "Get out, Perrone. If you have any ounce of decency in you, get out."

"Certainly. May the best man win." He looked right at Keenan, who clearly got flustered and out of sorts. After all, they had tried to get him to take a fall. Round five. That was the magic number to the bookies. They said Terry wouldn't last past the fifth round against Jake, whose conditioning was said to be in top form and who had a good left hook.

Perrone turned. The bodyguards opened the door for him, closing rank around the coward. Before he shut the door behind him, he turned and looked me in the eye. "You feel safe around here, Jack?"

"Of course I do, asshole."

"Hmm. Because I hear tales of muggings in Vegas. Car jackings. Would be a shame if anything happened to you. I hear you almost lost your spleen."

"It's okay."

"Had it been your liver, it would all have been over. Pity." And with that he closed the door.

All of us were shaken, not with fear, but rage. Sovo literally trembled as he fought to regain control. But I recognized that Terry needed to stay focused on Jake, not use all his adrenaline rush hating Perrone, who would one day go to prison, who wasn't worth our time.

Sovo had walked over to the far corner of the locker room. I could see him checking his weapon.

First, I talked to Terry. "Look, you can't let this guy send you over the top. Take a deep breath."

Terry did as I told him. "Terry, your adrenaline has to be saved for the fight. Don't waste it on him. Don't let him win. *You* win. You go past the five rounds. You go for all twelve rounds. Go the distance, Terry, and show the entire world what you're made of. This is for the fucking *heavyweight championship of the world*. And no matter what you do for the rest of your life, no one will ever be able to take it away from you. You'll be able to tell your children and grandchildren, and they'll be able to tell *their* children that you were the champ."

Terry looked right at me, and I saw the anger leave his eyes. He began to focus.

"All right, then. I'll be ringside. Win this one, Terry."

Sovo turned around and got ready to escort me to our seats. He patted Terry on the back a few times. "You win the title, Terry. Then I try to take it from you."

They smiled at each other, then Sovo and I left the locker room.

In the tunnel, I said to Sovo, "Can we find a quiet place to talk? How long until the fight?"

"One hour."

"Come on."

The Majestic had no fewer than twenty top restaurants and bars in it. The rooftop restaurant was the most elegant and the least noisy. It was away from the casino crowds. We rode up in a glass elevator and walked to the hostess stand. We told them we wanted to go into the bar, and the woman, in a long black evening gown, led the way and sat us at a small table near the window where we could gaze down on the neon of Las Vegas. In the distance, I saw the lights of the MGM Grand. We had fought there before.

"What is it, Jack?" Sovo looked at me with concern. I ordered a tequila with a lime wedge and Sovo ordered a Coke.

"Sovo, do we have a future together?"

He nodded. "It's all I want."

"I saw you in the locker room."

"What?" He looked puzzled.

I lowered my voice. "I saw you checking your weapon."

"But Perrone was there. He was antagonizing us."

"Exactly. He came into that locker room to intimidate. He came in there to throw Terry off his game. He came in there to frighten me. He came in there to make you throw your life away."

Sovo leaned back in his leather chair. The waitress brought us our drinks.

"What do you mean?"

"I mean, Sovo, that we have a shot at real happiness. The kind some people would give anything just to have a shot at. And if you pull that gun out in anger, when there's no *real* danger, just some intimidation, you will throw away this wonderful thing we have."

"But what if he tries to hurt you again?" He asked the question with the most innocent look on his face.

"Sovo," I whispered, "he's not going to turn his casino into a Wild West shooting gallery. He's looking to scare us, nothing more."

He looked down, and I reached out and outlined his face with my fingertip.

"Every time you touch me," he said, "I go crazy."

"Then listen to me. Please. You told me a sniper never wastes a shot."

"He doesn't."

"Then don't waste a single shot on Tony Perrone. Not one. Let him fall at trial. Let the feds bring him down. Let us go on with our lives."

He was quiet for a long, long time. I sipped my tequila and waited for him to speak. Finally, he said, "Okay."

"I care so much about you."

"I'll do as you ask."

We finished our drinks and then stood. "Come on, Sovo. It's fight time."

We left the restaurant and took the glass elevator

to the ground floor. It was time to see if Terry would be champion. If I had helped train a man who would rule as heavyweight champion of the world.

Chapter 26

Our seats were on one side of the ring, the exact opposite side from Tony Perrone. Benny Bonita was also there, maybe fifteen seats from Perrone. You could slice the tension with a Ginsu knife.

Both men had arrived with more bodyguards than usual, and security was very visible, with big men wearing secret-service-style earpieces roaming around. While there was the usual media frenzy about the fight, now the media was pressing them to give a comment on the charges being waged against them. Tony Perrone, who had long cultivated an image of respectability and class, bristled at each question. You could tell he hated the idea of being thought of as a criminal and common thug.

The media was also positing that this just might be the fight with the most venom ever between two fighters. Sure, Ali and Frazier had hated each other big time. There was an awful lot of trash talk. But Ali hadn't pistol-whipped Frazier's trainer. No, this would go down in the annals of the sport as the bitterest rivalry ever.

The ring announcer started his pronouncements. "In this corner, we have the challenger, from Las Vegas, Nevada, weighing 215 pounds, the Wild Irishman, with a record of thirty-two wins and one loss, Terry Keenan!"

The crowd roared its approval.

"And in this corner, hailing from Philadelphia, Pennsylvania, weighing a total of 225 pounds, and a record of twenty-nine wins and no losses, we have the current heavyweight champion of the world, Gentleman Jake Johnson."

I rolled my eyes at the excesses of nicknames in the boxing world. The reason they called Jake "Gentleman" was because he favored custom-made suits from Hong Kong and he never did an interview of any sort without being in a three-piece suit. In fact, the only time he was ever photographed out of his suits was at weigh-in and in the ring. So I guess, in boxing circles, where you've got to have a gimmick or a media image, Jake was "the Gentleman."

The crowd had also roared its approval for Jake. But the heavier applause was for Terry. I think the media storm surrounding Perrone and Bonita had soured people on their fighter a bit.

"Gentlemen," the ring referee said as the two fighters stood nose to nose. "I want a good clean fight. No hitting below the belt. When I say break, break. And may the best man win."

What he meant by that was sometimes fighters got all entangled and looked like wrestlers, then the ref would say "Break it up," and they were supposed to break it up. There were all sorts of rules in boxing. For instance, if a man falls to the canvas, in a knockout or potential knockout, the other man is supposed to go to a neutral corner.

I looked in Terry's corner. Deacon and Big Jimmy were there. Eddie stood there, too. I crossed my fingers for luck. Deacon looked excited. Not since his own championship days had he taken a fighter this far.

The bell signaled the start of round one. Both men looked good. Terry stuck to his game plan. He boxed instead of just slugging it out. He got in a lot of body shots, designed to make a man sore and tire him out. I was proud of how well he did and called encouragement into the ring. "Come on, Terry. Good job! Keep at him!"

Round two was more of the same. I called round one, in my mind, a toss-up. In round two, Terry was a bit more aggressive, so I gave that round to him.

Round three began and Terry saw an opening and delivered a solid left hook to Jake's jaw. Jake fell to the canvas, Terry retreated to a neutral corner, the crowd went wild, and the ref started counting, "One…two…three…" Jake was up by the count of four. So Terry had one knockdown to his credit, but Jake needed to *stay* down on the canvas to merit a *knockout*. Jake shook his head from side to side as if to clear it, and he came at Terry swinging. He landed a wild punch below the belt, which merited a penalty and an extra bit of rest for Terry in the corner.

"Not much fun getting a boxing glove in the balls," I said to Sovo.

"It's agony," he said, his face contorted with sympathy pain.

The fight resumed, and Jake was the aggressor, but with the one-point penalty, I considered the round a toss-up. The bell rang for the end of the round, and Jake landed one shot after the bell, meriting another warning, though they didn't take a point from him.

"This is shaping up to be an ugly fight," I said over the noise of the crowd.

Terry sat on the three-legged stool in the corner, while Big Jimmy rubbed a towel over him. He put his hand out and Terry spit out his mouth guard. Big Jimmy offered him a water bottle to sip from. Terry took a swig, swished it around and spit it into a bucket. Ah, the glamour of boxing. The mouth guard went back in, Terry stood and shadowboxed with energy, showing he wasn't tired, and then he moved to the center of the ring.

Round four opened with Terry getting a little sloppy. Maybe the after-the-bell punch, not to mention the shot to his testicles, had pissed him off, and he was trying to slug it out instead of using finesse and boxing like we told him. Deacon shouted from outside the ropes, "Box, Terry, box. Don't just swing at everything."

I looked across the ring and noticed Tony Perrone wasn't watching the match, he was staring at me—glaring, really. I hoped Sovo wouldn't notice, and, luckily, he was wrapped up in the match. In my mind, I had a flash of Perrone telling Tommy to go for my liver. He had wanted me dead. As a woman in a man's game, I was used to people resenting me. Hell, even Terry had been pissed the first time he met me and discovered Jack Rooney was actually "Jacqueline" Rooney. But I had never had anyone wish me real ill. Wish me dead. It was a disconcerting feeling, to say the least.

I tried to avoid looking over there and turned my attention to Terry. Because he was getting sloppy, he was taking some harsh body blows from Jake. The bell signaled the end of the round, and worriedly, I thought I would have to give the round to Jake.

Round five. Now, if Jake was on the take, then Perrone would have leaned on him to make sure, no matter what, that Terry went down by the end of the fifth round. That's what they had hoped to do by trying to bribe Terry and hold his brother's arrest over his head. Jake came out swinging like a man on a rampage. Terry defended well, and I realized, happily, that Jake was going to tire himself out. He was punching a lot more than he was landing. But then again, just one lucky shot to Terry's jaw and Terry could go down like a sack of potatoes.

Terry seemed to go back to our game plan. He settled down. He appeared to be enjoying irritating Jake. He danced and boxed and made funny faces to infuriate Jake. The more Terry frustrated him, the more desperate Jake looked. I glanced at the official ring clock, its digital numbers huge up on the wall.

"He just has to last thirty more seconds and Perrone loses big time," I said with glee. And Terry did just that, outlasting the round. I stood and clapped, my eyes focused on Perrone.

The remaining rounds seemed to flip-flop. One round was clearly won by Jake, the next by Terry. Finally, it was the last round, the twelfth. The thing about the twelfth round is it often comes down to endurance. By that round, both fighters are exhausted, sore, aching. Some fights end with them looking more like two marathon dancers, holding on to each other to keep from falling over.

When Terry first came to us, his endurance was shit. But we had built him up with long runs in the old canyons and on desert roads, as well as footwork exercises and jump rope. He was now a finely conditioned athlete.

Deacon leaned into him and whispered something

in his ear. Terry nodded and came out from his corner energized and swinging hard.

Jake tried to defend himself from the onslaught of punches. The crowd rose to its collective feet, and every voice seemed to shout as one, Ter-ry, Ter-ry, Ter-ry. Ter-ry. The chanting grew deafening. I looked around. Terry had to be rejuvenated having a huge crowd adoringly shouting his name. The crowd kept at it, caught up in the excitement.

And then, as long as I live, I'll never forget it. As if in slow motion, Terry drew his left arm back, and *bam!* He struck Jake square on the jaw, and Jake toppled backward, not even spreading his arms out to break his fall. His body bounced on the canvas. He was out cold, face upturned, eyes shut. The ref counted to ten.

One-two-three-four-five-six-seven-eight-nine-ten.

But Jake wasn't getting up. If the ref counted to a *hundred* he wasn't getting back up. The ref walked over to Terry and lifted one arm up. "The winner!"

Terry did it. He scored a *knockout!*

Chapter 27

The entire arena went wild. All except for Bonita and Perrone. Terry had his arms hoisted in the air, and he was jumping up and down. Deacon was hugging Big Jimmy and Big Jimmy was hugging Eddie and everyone was hugging Terry.

Terry's face began scanning the crowd. He locked onto me and Sovo and motioned with us to climb into the ring for the victory celebration. I wasn't sure I could do it, as banged up as I was, but Deacon and Big Jimmy parted the ropes, and Sovo gently lifted me up and helped me climb into the ring.

"You did it, Terry," I screamed over the noise.

"No, *we* did it!"

"You came out in the twelfth round like a real champ. Like Ali, like Foreman, like all the greats. What did Deacon say to you before the twelfth?"

Terry looked down at me and smiled. "He said, 'Win this for Jack.'"

The ring announcer came to the middle of the ring and, handing Terry the three belts of the unified heavyweight championship, declared, "The winner, by knockout in the twelfth round, is Wild Irishman Terry Keenan."

Terry held his belts aloft for the crowd to see and admire and cheer. He paced from one end of the ring to the other, enjoying his moment of glory. Pandemonium still reigned in the seats. The pay-per-view announcers had climbed into the ring and began interviewing Terry. Flashbulbs went off in every direction.

The announcer said, "Terry, or shall I call you Champ now? An awful lot of commotion has been happening around you as you prepared for this fight. Your trainer, Jack Rooney, was seriously injured in what appears to be criminal circumstances. You were all distracted by the very serious situation surrounding you. How were you able to push it aside and come here and win the heavyweight championship of the world?"

"Well, Gil, Jack Rooney is standing right over there, and she was an inspiration to me. Any time I felt tired, any time I hurt, any time I felt a bit of self-doubt, I only had to think of her ordeal and know I could do it."

"Jack Rooney, can you come on camera, please?" Gil motioned to me.

I had talked to Gil a hundred times before. I wasn't keen at being on national television with facial bruising like the damn Elephant Man, but I moved over to them.

"Jack, what do you have to say about your fighter here?"

"Gil, he did an amazing job. He stuck to the game plan, he trained hard, he was in peak physical condition. He was truly amazing, and he really deserves all the credit for that."

"Jack, your injuries are quite visible. How are you doing?"

"Beating Benny Bonita's man in the ring was the best medicine I could ask for."

"Terry, back to you. You realize that the next logical fight would be against your sparring partner and friend, the man they call the Kosovo Killer. How do you feel about that?"

"Hey, I had my shot, and if Sovo is next, then I'll fight him." Sovo came over and wrapped an arm around Terry's shoulder, the two of them beaming.

"Any words for Jake Johnson? Is a rematch possible?"

"It's premature to talk rematch. Right now I want to enjoy my championship, my win. This is my night. This is my team's night."

"You heard it here, folks. Drawing his inspiration from his trainer, Terry Keenan takes the heavyweight championship of the world. On New Year's Eve. And I bet this is going to be a helluva year for him."

The ring announcer next declared that it was two minutes to midnight. Looking at the Jumbotrons throughout the arena, we watched as the countdown began. As midnight loomed, the crowd chanted together, "Ten-nine-eight-seven-six-five-four-three-two-one! Happy New Year!" as confetti rained from the ceiling and balloons fell on us in the colors of royal blue and gold—the Majestic's theme colors.

I turned to Sovo, who tenderly bent down and kissed me. Every time he kissed me, it felt as if my body was on fire. There among thousands, it was no different. The rest of the world just faded away.

We stayed in the ring and gave interviews. Sovo was interviewed by a number of different television stations. Deacon gave a bunch of interviews. I gave a couple. After the crowd had dissipated, we were led to the press room for a formal press conference.

A long table was lined up at one end of the room, and there were seats for our entire team. The room was wall-to-wall media, with the photographers kneeling in front so they could get their pictures. We answered questions from reporters as far away as Japan, as well as reporters from *Sports Illustrated, The New York Times* and all the top American media. Bulbs flashed in our eyes. We stayed for about forty minutes, trying to be gracious as question after question brought up Bonita, Perrone, the tapes and so on. Everyone was careful to use the word *alleged*. In the end, we started saying that questions like that would be deferred to our attorney. This was Terry's night, and I wanted to rightly put the focus back on him.

We went back to our locker room to collect our things. "So, champ, you going out to celebrate?" I asked.

"Nah. I want to go home to the ranch."

"What? You've been in virtual lockdown there for a month. No wild women? No drunken binges? No scandals tonight?" I teased. "I bet there are a hundred women in this place who would go off with the heavyweight champion of the world in a heartbeat."

"You know, I don't have it in me right now. The only people I want to celebrate with are my *real* friends. All you guys."

"Well, don't be surprised if I pass out on you. I'm so exhausted, I can barely keep my eyes open."

He smiled at me, and we all left the locker room. The only people in the tunnel were a couple of straggling reporters with press passes on them. I was surprised they were allowed down the tunnel, but it was late, and I guess Security figured what the hell. We nodded at the reporters and walked toward the exit.

As we made our way out of the tunnel, Tony Perrone appeared, again with his big bodyguards.

I felt Sovo tighten next to me. But for some reason, I was unafraid. Perrone had dished out the worst to me, and I had taken it and survived. I assumed maybe some time in the future, I might have a moment, or a day, where what I went through would haunt me or frighten me. Some day, I would have nightmares of the hard concrete coming up to meet my face. But for now, I was empowered by having survived.

"You know, Jack, your fighter here has cost a lot of people a lot of money."

I moved to the front of our pack. "No. *Your* fighter, by losing, cost a lot of people a lot of money. And that's the way the game goes. It's 'may the best man win,' not 'may the man who's accepted the biggest bribe win.'"

"We're not through, you know."

"Oh, yes we are. Those tapes will ruin you. They'll bring you down and put you away for a long, long time. And what those tapes don't do, my testimony will. Do you know, in the hospital, they came in when I was unconscious and took five rolls of film? Every fucking bruise, every swollen knuckle. You won't get away with this, Perrone. Not this time. You're looking at thirty years. Attempted murder, kidnapping, racketeering. You know, Perrone, you'll likely die in prison."

Without warning, Perrone drew a gun and pointed it right at me. "If I'm going away, I might as well finish what I started."

Sovo withdrew his gun, and I turned my head to him and pleaded with him not to. "Don't, Sovo."

Perrone sneered, "Seems we have a standoff."

"Put it away, Perrone," Terry said. "Look, you do some time, you're done with it. Time off for good behavior. You kill someone and that's it. Think clearly for a change."

"You know, Jack, according to Benny Bonita, you're just like your mother."

As I was opening my mouth to tell him to shut the fuck up, he raised his gun. I screamed and then I heard a gun go off.

I wasn't hit, but Tony Perrone was. In the chest. Dead center. Dead…period.

I looked over at Sovo, who shook his head at me. I looked at his gun, which was at his side. I hugged him. He hadn't fired. But who had?

"All right, folks, Federal Bureau of Investigation." The four "reporters" who were straggling in the tunnel suddenly pulled out wallets with gold, shiny badges in them.

"Boy, am I ever glad to see you guys."

The FBI had their guns drawn and trained on Perrone's bodyguards, who all had their hands raised in the air.

One agent leaned down. "One less sack of shit to worry about," he said as he felt for a pulse.

Next thing I knew, the bodyguards were being frisked, we were giving statements, and some time later, we were walking out of the Majestic Casino into the night air of Las Vegas, finally through with Tony Perrone.

"Happy New Year," Sovo said to me, as he helped me undress.

"Happy New Year," I said, yawning.

He stripped and then we both slid into my bed. Never before had my goose-down comforter felt so good. We opened the window and let the night air in.

"How do you feel?" he asked.

"I took a painkiller. Sore, achy, but so happy. I trained a heavyweight champion, Sovo."

"You know," he said, "thank you for what you said to me in the bar. I think, for a long time now, I'm some kind of monster. But you show me I'm not."

I yawned. "Good night, Sovo." I slid over and rested my head on his chest.

"Good night, Jack," he whispered. And sometime after that, I fell asleep and dreamed of Sovo and me in the mountains of Kosovo, overlooking his village, and eating hearty bread and drinking wine. My father was there. And Deacon. Big Jimmy. Destiny. Crystal. Sovo's sister. Everyone. And it was peaceful. And beautiful. And three white doves flew overhead.

It was a very good dream.

Chapter 28

Sovo, Deacon and I waited outside the penitentiary.

My wounds were all healed. Latest CAT scan showed my skull healing nicely. My ribs were better. My face just had a touch of bruising and cover-up took care of it.

The gates opened, a buzzer sounded, and my father marched out into our waiting arms. Tears flowed freely. I used to be afraid to show my emotions, but not anymore. Not after all we went through—each of us.

"God, it's so good just to touch you and see you face-to-face, without some prison guard standing over my shoulder." He looked back at the prison. At the four corners of the yard were tall watchtowers with guards with rifles pacing back and forth. I shuddered to think of him in that place.

"Amen, sweet Jesus. Sean, it's good to have you home!" Deacon gave him a bear hug.

Sovo shook his hand and then my father pulled Sovo to him, and said, "Thank you for taking such good care of my daughter."

We took the long drive back to the ranch. Me and my father sat in the back; Deacon drove, and Sovo sat in the passenger seat. Mama Bear had made my father a small picnic basket for the ride, filled with his favorite foods: fried chicken, brownies and a nice cold beer. He sighed as he enjoyed each treat—especially the beer.

When we reached the ranch, my father was like a little kid, his head popping up over the seat and then looking out the windows, trying to catch a glimpse of the place.

"The ranch hasn't changed much, has it?" my father asked.

"Well, it's changed a little," I said.

"How so?"

"You know, we don't spend much time at the house near the city anymore. Deacon and me. We're out here ninety percent of the time. We like it here. It's peaceful. And after all we've experienced, a little peace and quiet is very nice."

"Oh, and one more thing," Deacon said.

"What's that?"

I knew what Deacon was thinking. "Look over there." I pointed to the left of the house.

My father rubbed his eyes. "Is that a...pony?"

"Destiny's gotten a little spoiled," I said. "The horse's name is Mr. Wiggle."

"And how's the little angel doing?"

"Really well. We sent her to a grief counselor. She's just starting to deal with Crystal's death, but Mama Bear and Big Jimmy are just great with her."

We parked the car and climbed out. My father was very pale from prison, but a few days out in the desert would restore the color to his cheeks.

As my father walked into the house, Big Jimmy came and clasped him in an embrace. Mama Bear, who'd moved in and taken over the cooking, came out from the kitchen wearing an apron, and Destiny was with her, wearing a little apron of her own.

"Destiny..." I leaned down. "Remember when I told you my father was a good guy and I couldn't wait for you to meet him?"

She nodded.

"Well, here he is. You can call him Uncle Sean."

Destiny shyly stepped forward and then ran and gave my father a hug. He knelt down and let her look into his eyes.

"Hey, princess."

"Hi." She placed her tiny hands on each side of his face and rubbed his face.

"Come on. I cooked a big turkey. You hungry?" Mama Bear asked him.

"Ravenous for something other than institutional food. Thanks for the picnic basket. It hit the spot."

We all sat at the big oak table in the kitchen, and Deacon said grace. For the first time in years, my family—admittedly a hodgepodge of people—was all together under one roof.

As Deacon would say, "Praise the Lord."

Fourteen months later, Benny Bonita drew a thirty-five-year prison sentence. In fact, the entire case took down dozens in the Vegas police department and in the Mob.

I testified in court against him, and also the body-guard who beat me, as well as the fake FBI agent. I told the story over and over again, which was cathartic. And after a while, we didn't care what happened to Bonita. We were moving on to better times.

Which is why, with my father home, I agreed to marry Sovo.

Originally, I thought we would get married by Elvis. I didn't care. I just wanted my father to walk me down the aisle. It could have been the aisle of a plane for all I cared.

But Deacon? He had other plans, which included officiating at our wedding. "I have no children," he told me, "so you're it, and if you think, in your crazy, stubborn little mind, that you're going to deprive me of the chance to marry you two, you've gone and lost it. It's all that junk food you eat."

So we decided to get married out at the ranch. We

erected two big white tents, one for the ceremony and one for the small reception. We brought in potted, blooming plants, and the place smelled like jasmine and orange blossoms. Destiny was the flower girl, which was better, she told me, than getting "all the Barbies in the world." Actually, the way Big Jimmy spoils her, I'm not sure that she doesn't have all the Barbies in the world to begin with. And Sovo asked Terry to be the best man. I laughed, remembering the time they came to real blows in the ring. Now they were inseparable.

I found the concept of a virginal white dress rather…silly. So I opted instead for a vintage dress from the 1940s, off-white with tiny white roses hand-sewn into the chiffon and beading on the bodice. Instead of a veil, I wore white lilies of the valley and white roses woven into my hair, which I pinned into a loose chignon with curls falling around my face. When I looked in the mirror and smiled, my cheek, which had been shattered, gave me a dimpled appearance on one side. The plastic surgeon wanted to fix it, but you know, as horrific as our ordeal was, it was in those hotel rooms, on the run, that I think I fell in love.

Destiny and I stood in my room.

"You look beautiful, Auntie Jack."

"You think so?"

"Mmm-hmm. Do you think my mommy is here? In spirit?"

We had taken to telling Destiny that Crystal was all around us, and in many ways, I felt she was.

"Of course I do. That's why I don't have a maid of honor. If she was here, I would ask her to be. So I think of her being here in spirit."

"Is it okay to miss her so much my heart hurts sometimes? 'Cause it does, you know."

"Sure. I do know. And I miss her sometimes so much *my* heart hurts."

"And is it also okay to be so happy sometimes that I feel like my heart…like it's up in the sky?"

"That, too."

My father came and knocked on the door. He was wearing a freshly pressed black suit, crisp white shirt and a bolo tie. He also had on his favorite pair of black cowboy boots. He'd gained about fifteen pounds since he got home, eating every single food he had missed while he was locked away. The weight looked good on him.

"Jack…you look gorgeous."

"Yeah, well don't let that get around. People might not take me seriously as a boxing trainer."

"I don't think there's any danger of that." And indeed, there wasn't. My story made *Sports Illustrated*, and Deacon and I now had more fame and boxers than we could handle. And of course, Sovo would be fighting Terry in a month. I trained Sovo; Deacon trained Terry. But they still sparred. They'd agreed that whatever the outcome, they would be cool with it.

Dad, Destiny and I walked through the house to the front porch. From there, they had laid down a white carpet made of a silky fabric for me as an aisle. A real aisle that my father could walk me down. Under the white tent was the whole camp, a slew of former motorcycle-club members, the gun dealer who'd kept us well supplied, and even two FBI agents and a D.A. And Claire, my nurse, who, no matter how much she and Deacon tried to deny, was sweet on him and vice versa.

We hired a violinist, who began to play a Vivaldi piece, and first Destiny walked, just like we practiced, carrying her basket and scattering rose petals. Big Jimmy beamed and wiped at his eyes with a crisp white handkerchief from the pocket of his suit jacket. Then my father and I began to walk down the aisle. I patted his arm several times, as if I couldn't quite believe he was there.

And at the end of the aisle, standing underneath an arbor they'd made for us, was Sovo. He had on a dress gray suit with a dark blue tie. His hair was freshly cut, and he was clean-shaven and smiling. It was as if the grief he always carried with him was finally lifted, like a fog burning off in the sun.

In my mind, like my life flashing before my eyes, I pictured a man who was wounded inside, but who learned that once a killer, not always a killer. I even pictured the moment I shot Rob. Wherever he was, I was certain he was sorry. But it was too late, and I refused to weep for him.

And I pictured my Sovo. The way he made love to me. The way he held my hand. The way, when the sunset was especially pretty, he would look the other way, I think because the emotions got too strong.

My father kissed me and then shook Sovo's hand. I stood next to him. Deacon's voice resonated as he went through the traditional ceremony. He read from Corinthians on the meaning of love, how it is patient and kind.

When it was finally time to say I do and kiss the bride, there wasn't a dry eye in the house.

After we kissed, we turned around and I spotted Destiny. She waved to me and tossed more rose petals. Her mother was right to name her Destiny.

For one tiny little girl had changed all of our lives.

* * * * *

Books by Erica Orloff

Silhouette Bombshell

Urban Legend #8
Knockout #19

ATHENA FORCE

Chosen for their talents.
Trained to be the best.

Expected to change the world.

The women of Athena Academy
share an unforgettable experience
and an unbreakable bond—until
one of their own is murdered.

The adventure begins with these six books:

PROOF by Justine Davis, July 2004

ALIAS by Amy J. Fetzer, August 2004

EXPOSED by Katherine Garbera,
September 2004

DOUBLE-CROSS by Meredith Fletcher,
October 2004

PURSUED by Catherine Mann, November 2004

JUSTICE by Debra Webb, December 2004

**And look for six more Athena Force stories
January to June 2005.**

Available at your favorite retail outlet.

Bestselling fantasy author Mercedes Lackey turns traditional fairy tales on their heads in the land of the Five Hundred Kingdoms.

Elena, a Cinderella in the making, gets an unexpected chance to be a Fairy Godmother. But being a Fairy Godmother is hard work and she gets into trouble by changing a prince who is destined to save the kingdom, into a donkey—but he really deserved it!

Can she get things right and save the kingdom?
Or will her stubborn desire to teach this ass of a prince a lesson get in the way?

On sale November 2004.
Visit your local bookseller.

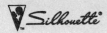

Silhouette®

BOMBSHELL™

COMING NEXT MONTH

#21 SISTER OF FORTUNE—Lindsay McKenna
Sisters of the Ark

An ancient artifact had plagued Vicky Mabrey's dreams
for a year, and now she had to find it—with the help of
an enemy from her past. Vicky couldn't stand the sight of
Griff Hutchinson, but they had to work together to find the precious crystal—before it fell into the wrong hands and destroyed
the people Vicky loved.

#22 JUSTICE—Debra Webb
Athena Force

Her best friend's killer was dead, and so was police lieutenant
Kayla Ryan's best lead to find her friend's missing child. Now
Kayla had to work with a lethally sexy detective to find the person who'd sent the assassin, and to bring him to justice.
But she couldn't shake the feeling that someone was watching
her every move.... Was the enemy closer than she'd ever sus-
pected?

#23 NIGHT LIFE—Katherine Garbera

Sasha Malone Sterling had given up the dark life of a spy to
be a wife and mother. But the agency had called her back
for a mission she couldn't refuse: bringing in a rogue agent.
She was the only one who could catch him—because the
agent was Sasha's own estranged husband, and no one
knew him better than she did.

#24 HOT CASE—Patricia Rosemoor

Detective and confirmed skeptic Shelley Caldwell couldn't have
been more different from her naive twin sister. But when her
twin found a body, drained of blood, that later disappeared,
Shelley was eerily reminded of an old case that still haunted
her. The old trail was heating fast—and to follow it, Shelley
would trade places with her twin and enter the dark world of
Goths, wannabe vampires and maybe even the real deal.

SBCNM1104